A LESSON IN LOVE

Attractive widow Carol meets Paul on a campsite in France. After her return from holiday she discovers that he is the new tutor at her art class. Their friendship develops but, suspecting Paul may already have a partner, she is reluctant to make a commitment. During a visit to her health club, company director Simon introduces himself and later wines and dines her. Torn between the two, it takes a dangerous encounter for her to acknowledge her true love.

Books by Shirley Heaton
in the Linford Romance Library:

CHANCE ENCOUNTER

SHIRLEY HEATON

◆

A LESSON IN LOVE

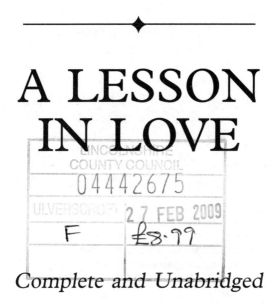

Complete and Unabridged

LINFORD
Leicester

First published in Great Britain in 2007

First Linford Edition
published 2008

British Library CIP Data

Heaton, Shirley
 A lesson in love.—Large print ed.—
 Linford romance library
 1. Triangles (Interpersonal relations)—
 Fiction 2. Love stories 3. Large type books
 I. Title
 823.9′2 [F]

 ISBN 978–1–84782–149–2

Published by
F. A. Thorpe (Publishing)
Anstey, Leicestershire

Set by Words & Graphics Ltd.
Anstey, Leicestershire
Printed and bound in Great Britain by
T. J. International Ltd., Padstow, Cornwall

This book is printed on acid-free paper

1

His face said it all. Carol smiled and held out her arms. 'It's not the end of the world, Josh. Don't look so glum.'

Josh came towards her. She reached up and ruffled his fair hair. It was five days to his sixteenth birthday, yet he towered over her. Just like his dad.

A familiar sadness descended, and she pulled Josh towards her, momentarily holding him close. The memories flooded back. Since that fateful day eight years ago when Mike had been involved in a car crash Carol had coped alone. Mike was a careful driver, but he had no chance with a maniac on the road. The other driver, an alcoholic, was too far gone and should never have been driving.

At the time hurt, sadness and absolute fury possessed Carol, almost pushing her over the edge, but she had to remain sane for the sake of Josh. He was only seven and, during those formative years, he needed his daddy more than ever. How she dragged herself though the ordeal and survived unscathed, she would never know.

She shook herself back to the present. A shimmer of warmth flowed through her and her mood quickly changed. Gently pushing him to arms length, she said, 'What happened? Come on, love tell me.'

'My results, I've blown it, Mum. Three Cs and a D, I needed four Cs.'

'I'm sure they'll accept you back, Josh. We'll go into school together after the holidays.'

'But they don't cater for re-sits. I can't go back to school.'

He was so disappointed with his results, she felt for him. He'd set his mind on staying on at school to study for an advanced diploma. Surely they would find a way.

'How about college?' she suggested, her huge brown eyes shining with optimism. 'I have a prospectus some-where,' she continued, reaching over to her letter rack and rustling through papers. 'I think I popped it in here'. She drew out an envelope and handed it to him. 'Here it is. I'm sure they'll sort something out. We'll call in and see what they have to offer.'

'But I won't know anyone at college.' His blue eyes searched hers, a deep frown sketching his forehead.

'Don't worry. It'll be a fresh start and you'll soon make friends.'

She shuddered as vivid memories came to mind of the problems she'd faced when she lost Mike. Josh had clung to her and refused to go to school. It had taken a great deal of time and a lot of love and affection to persuade him to go back.

'But let's not think about that now. We have the holiday to look forward to. I suggest we pop into town this afternoon. You need a couple of T-shirts, and I'm desperately in need of a new bikini,' she said, rolling her eyes in an exaggerated way.

After lunch they set off for town. Carol was convinced she could still get away with a bikini, even though lots of women in their late thirties were now wearing one-piece swimsuits. Thanks to her membership at *Images*, the health club in the village, she was slim and her figure was in good shape.

And what a boon the club had been. At first, she'd thought it was too expensive, but working from home it was easy to slot in a couple of extra hours each week to cover the cost. Provided she completed the conveyances on time, she was a free agent.

The afternoon shopping trip was fruitful. She found the T-shirts for Josh and she bought a bikini in readiness for the holiday in France.

By the following Friday afternoon she'd completed the last of the conveyances. She shut down the computer and took her car into the village to the solicitors, Barron and Weeks, where she dropped off the documents.

That was it. No more work for two weeks.

It was early Saturday morning when Carol drove to Dover to catch the ferry across to Calais. Mike would have been proud that she'd become sufficiently experienced to drive on the continent. It was certainly the best way to have a sunshine holiday abroad on her limited budget.

Josh was sitting beside her, map in hand ready to navigate, something she'd encouraged since he was twelve years old. He would mark the route beforehand, she would check it through and, with a little supervision he was responsible for getting them there.

The port at Dover was bustling with travellers when they arrived and they queued for over an hour before driving on to the ferry. The crossing was rough and they had very little sleep, but they were in Calais by early morning.

'Ready for the off, Mum?' Josh was well prepared and raring to go.

'Point me in the right direction,' she

said, slipping her arm around his shoulder and squeezing him. 'You're the boss!'

The mist lingered over the fields as they set off south, but it soon dispersed, the bright sunshine casting its glow on the rich, green pastures. The beautiful countryside steeped in peace and tranquillity gave Carol an immense feeling of gratitude that, despite losing Mike at such a young age, she still had Josh.

She took a sidelong glance and her heart tumbled with love for him as she watched him concentrating on his map-reading.

'Is it time to stop for lunch yet?' she asked, giving him a beam of a smile. 'I'm ravenously hungry.'

'Don't be impatient, Mum,' he said in a grown-up way as though reprimanding her. He smiled impishly. 'We'll stop on the outskirts of Amiens in ten minutes or so, have lunch and carry on to the site outside Paris.'

'Sounds good. Perhaps when we've

pitched the tent we could take the train into Paris like we did a couple of years ago and do a little early evening window shopping.'

'That's fine by me, Mum.'

It was another fifteen minutes before they came across a little café where they sat outside under a gaily-coloured parasol. They ordered baguettes filled with cheese and salad, and freshly bottled spring water.

'This is the life,' Carol said, stretching her legs and relaxing after the long drive. 'I could stay here all day.' But she knew they must move on if they were to keep their schedule.

'That was good,' she declared as she dabbed her face with the napkin. 'I think I can face it now. Paris here we come.' She paused for thought and after a moment or two she turned to Josh and said, 'It won't be long before you're helping me with the driving. You can send for your provisional licence now you're sixteen, but you can't start until you're seventeen.'

'Wow, me helping with the driving. I can't wait.' He grabbed her hand and pulled her towards him, popping a kiss on her cheek.

By the time they reached the site, Carol was exhausted. 'Do you mind if we give the trip to Paris a miss? The journey's got to me. I'm bushed.'

'I don't mind at all, Mum. I wasn't fussed about going there anyway. It was for your sake really, for you to look in the shops and see what you could buy if you had the money.' He laughed and then his face became serious. 'Once I get myself settled into a job, I'm going to treat you to something really nice.'

'You don't have to buy me anything, love. I'm happy as I am, you know that.'

They pitched the tent and Carol slept soundly that night. She awoke early next morning to the sound of the cows in the adjacent field. Stretching her arms, she yawned and peered across to where Josh should have been. His sleeping bag was empty. She pulled herself up from the ground, slipped on her jeans and sweater and peeped out through the tent flaps. He was making tea and cooking breakfast. The morning air was cool, but up above the sun was pushing its way through the clouds.

'Those sausages smell good,' she called out.

'Don't they just,' he said, smiling. 'I was so hungry this morning I had to get things started. Stay there. I'll bring you a cuppa.'

They left the site, this time heading for St. Etienne. Josh reckoned if they could make it there before the light started to fade, they could tackle the final leg of their journey the following day.

It was mid-afternoon two days later when they finally entered the site just outside St. Tropez. Carol knew things would be starting to trail off now that it was nearing the end of August when, within a couple of weeks, the schools would be starting a new term. The temperature was soaring even as they arrived, and her first priority after pitching the tent was to have a cool, refreshing shower.

'That's better,' she murmured as she made her way from the shower block back to the tent, now taking in the people around her.

To one side was a couple Carol guessed to be in their thirties with what seemed to be a horde of children, maybe five or six of them all together. She smiled as the little ones chased one another around the site, and she sadly reflected how she would have loved another child of her own. But that wasn't to be.

To the other side there were several tents in a cluster, apparently housing a party of grown-ups. One of the women waved and came across to introduce herself.

'I'm Liz Wentworth,' she said. 'We're all regulars from the north of England. Where are you from?' she asked.

'We're from Leeds,' she replied. 'I'm Carol Henderson and this is my son, Josh.'

'I must say, you don't look old enough to have a son his size,' Liz commented looking Josh up and down, and grinning. 'How about joining us this evening? You too, Josh.'

Josh nodded and smiled shyly as he picked up the huge water flagon. 'I'll fill this, Mum,' he said and he headed down the field.

That evening they dressed in casual wear and popped across to Liz's tent with a bottle of red wine.

'Hi,' Carol called to a couple who were cooking steaks on a barbecue nearby. 'Carol and Josh,' she said, holding out her hand.

The woman turned to her. 'Liz told us about you. I'm Julie,' she reciprocated and, pointing to the man beside her she added, 'my husband, Simon.'

He smiled, taking Carol's hand and shaking it vigorously. 'Take a seat. Have you eaten?'

'We have actually. I hope we're not disturbing anything. I didn't realise you wouldn't be eating until later.'

'We're free and easy here, however the mood takes us.'

Several other campers mostly in their thirties and forties turned up, some in couples, but it wasn't easy for Carol to decide how they paired off.

Minutes later a young man in his teens tapped Josh on the shoulder. 'Hi there, I'm Tom. Fancy a game of table tennis in the centre,' he said, pointing to the communal building.

Josh looked up. 'Great!' he said, nodding his agreement. 'By the way, I'm Josh,' and turning to Carol he added, 'you don't mind do you, Mum?'

But before she could reply, Tom grinned and whispered to Josh, 'I'm sure she doesn't, I've left the old man by himself over there.' He pointed to one of the tents. 'They'll manage, don't worry.'

Carol overheard and smiled to herself. Who was in charge of their party? The way Tom spoke it was obviously not the 'old man', more likely Tom himself. How long before Josh took charge?

Josh stood up ready to leave, but she tapped him on his arm. 'I heard that,' she said laughing. 'He's right. I'm sure the 'old lady' will be fine without you.'

Josh grinned. 'You said that, not me,' he said and Carol watched him follow Tom to his tent where they appeared to be having a conversation with the man sitting outside. Afterwards they wandered off down the slope towards the building.

It was a relief that Josh had accepted Tom's invitation. Carol had realised that most of the group were adults and she had begun to worry that Josh would be bored and feel left out. But once Tom was on the scene she knew she had no cause to fret.

One or two more campers came along and introduced themselves. They seemed a lively crowd, smiling and ready for fun. Julie passed her a glass of wine.

'You did say red, didn't you, Carol?'

'I did. That's lovely, Julie. Thanks,' she said and she took a sip thinking how lucky they were to have made friends so quickly.

But she was aroused from her thoughts by a voice from behind her. 'So you're the 'old lady'.'

Taken aback, she turned her head. There standing behind her was a man she guessed to be about her age. She stared at him and he stared straight back at her. Her knees felt weak and her heart began to flutter. He was drop-dead gorgeous.

'I've heard all about you,' he continued. 'I take it you've been given the night off too. Aren't we the lucky ones?'

She continued to stare, unable to draw herself away. Surely he couldn't be 'the old man'? He looked anything but old to her. Tall with a thatch of blond hair which fell in a sweep across his forehead, he moved closer, sitting beside her, his magnificent blue eyes burning into hers and totally transfixing her.

An unexpected frisson of warmth

seemed to glow within her. She gulped and her stomach flipped in a somersault. Pulling her gaze away from him, she averted her eyes.

'Let me introduce myself,' he said. 'Paul Trent, alias 'the old man'!' He laughed and took her hand, holding it firmly in his and shaking it. He looked her up and down, and she caught a satisfied glint in his eye. 'Now I don't recall having seen you here before.' He squeezed her hand.

She stuttered, 'Carol Henderson. You're right. We've not been to this site before. And yes, I am 'the old lady', not that I feel my age,' she added, covering her mouth to stifle a giggle, the tell-tale flush of embarrassment rising to her cheeks.

She couldn't remember the last time she'd blushed. Surely she could keep her calm? She was thirty-eight years old for goodness sake!

Letting go of his hand she took a deep breath, allowing herself time to recover her composure. She didn't normally go to pieces when someone flattered her. But . . .

A pinprick of guilt flickered inside her. This was becoming too cosy. She had always said she would never become involved again after she lost Mike. He was the only man she could ever love. Anything else would be shallow. And the loss had been too painful for her ever to want to experience again.

But why was she thinking in this vein? The guy hadn't asked her to marry him or anything so drastic. He was merely introducing himself. This was nothing but an informal gathering, a bit of fun, and she could relish a dollop of that.

'They seem to have hit it off — the boys I mean.' Paul cut into her thoughts. He paused, 'They obviously don't want us around. Granted Tom's seventeen, almost eighteen now. Maybe next year, he'll go off with his mates. What will I do then?' he joked and she felt herself drawn once more to those wonderful sparkling eyes.

A convulsive shiver ran down her spine. Was he intimating he needed a soul-mate? But she was reading into his words a message she had obviously conjured up through a figment of her imagination. Either that or it was wishful thinking.

'I know what you mean. Josh is just sixteen. But it won't be long before he wants to fly the nest.' Her stomach churned at the thought.

'I see you've already introduced yourself, Paul.' It was Liz who sat down next to them and smiled. 'You say you haven't been to this site before, Carol. Where do you usually go?'

'We come to Provence. We love this corner of the world. But this is the furthest south we've ventured.'

'We love it here too,' she replied. 'I'm pleased Tom's gone off with Josh. They're of a similar age, I gather. In the early days we all brought our children, but Tom is one of the youngest. He's going to university soon. He'll probably not be with us next year,' she added. 'Now let me introduce you to the others.'

Carol met the rest of the group by which time, much to her disappointment, Paul had wandered off and was chatting to some of the men. He hadn't mentioned a wife or a partner, but maybe if one existed they each had separate holidays. Couples sometimes preferred to holiday apart, believing it was good for the partnership.

'By the end of the evening Paul came across to say goodnight. He took her hand and pulled her towards him pensively, and his breath touched her cheek. 'Goodnight, Carol,' he said, popping a gentle kiss on her forehead. Her pulses started to pound again and the blood surged through her veins.

But, knowing she mustn't let herself be carried away, she gratefully retreated towards the tent before risking another glance at him. And when she did, he was looking back at her. She dashed inside the tent and when she scrambled into her sleeping bag she found it hard to erase his image from her mind. She hadn't come on holiday to find herself a man. And in any case, anyone she became involved with would have to have Josh's seal of approval. He was her first priority.

Disappointingly, during the next few days Carol saw little of Paul. It seemed he went off each day and didn't return until late evening. During those times his conversations were light-hearted, but brief and often shared with others. Whatever the reason for his absence during the day, Carol found herself waiting for his return, hoping they'd meet up in the evening to continue their banter. That's all it was, innocent banter but good fun.

Towards the second week of the holiday, she was beginning to realise she was living in fantasyland. What was wrong with her? She was behaving like teenager. Her own son would have had a more mature approach.

Up at first light, Carol left Josh in his

sleeping bag undisturbed. Collecting the flagon to replenish the water, she took a short cut and walked across the field. The grass was damp and once or twice she almost slipped, but she managed to stay upright. All was quiet and, as she turned to set off back, she was surprised to see Paul emerging from the men's shower area.

'Let me carry that,' he called out, taking the flagon from her. 'Be careful across the field,' he added. 'It's quite slippery.' Taking her hand he clasped it firmly and tucked it under his arm, causing a sensation of pleasure to ripple over her skin. She shuddered and hoped he hadn't noticed.

'Thanks, Paul. You're up early this morning,' she replied as he led her back.

'It was one of those nights. I just couldn't sleep,' he said, still holding her hand.

I know the feeling, she thought.

'When are you leaving for England?' she asked him. 'You've obviously been here much longer than we have.'

'Unfortunately, later this morning,' he said.

A twinge of disappointment gripped her.

'Did Tom mention he's starting university? He's not due there until the end of September, but I need to be back before then.'

'I see,' she said, wondering what Paul did for a living, but it was not in her nature to pry.

'I must say, you're up and about early yourself,' Paul observed.

'I like to make the best of the days. It's so relaxing, just going out and about. We're not leaving until next week,' she said as they reached her tent. She stretched out her hand for the flagon and he smiled, placing it on the ground beside her.

'I'm sorry you weren't here earlier,' he replied, his riveting gaze holding hers. 'I've enjoyed your company and I had hoped we could get to know each other a little better before I left, but time's been against me.' His gaze slid down to her mouth and she found herself holding her breath.

He took hold of her hand, leaned over and pecked her on each cheek. 'Maybe we'll meet again some time,' he added and then he disappeared inside his tent.

The unexpected compliment sent a shimmer of warmth right through her. He'd enjoyed being with her. But then she realised he was leaving and she felt deflated. She didn't even know where he lived. And why hadn't they seen more of each other?

He had said time had been against him. What did he mean by that? Wasn't he on holiday? Perhaps he had a job down here. Maybe that was why he wasn't around during the daytime. But she stopped herself from plucking silly ideas out of space. There was no mileage in it. He was leaving and that was that.

The second week came and went. It was equally enjoyable, but she had to admit to herself that she'd missed seeing Paul around. But it was time to leave and they had a long drive ahead of them, first back to the site outside Paris and eventually to Calais in time to catch their scheduled ferry.

Familiar with the strain of navigating, having been in that position when Mike was alive, Carol gave Josh an extra half hour to rest before his task began, whilst she started to pack her own things and prepare breakfast.

She lit the stove and placed the billycan on top. Her absolute priority was a cup of tea. She'd take one into Josh and let him come round gradually before packing.

They were away on time. The journey was monotonous and tiring. It was late afternoon on Sunday before she drew up outside the house.

'That's it. Over and done with for another year,' she said, stepping out of the car a feeling of sadness lingering inside, she didn't know why. But maybe she was fooling herself. Since leaving the camp site she'd been battling to rid her mind of the image of Paul Trent with those sparkling eyes and that flashing white smile.

2

'It's college enrolment next week.' Josh mumbled the words, his face a solemn mask.

'It'll be an exciting new venture,' Carol replied brightly.

'I don't know, Mum,' he replied, his voice matching the look on his face.

'Well I do, love. You'll be fine,' she continued, determined to be positive. Now I'll put the kettle on if you'll bring the bags in,' she said changing the subject.

She smiled and dropped the teabags into the teapot. 'When you've got a minute, take a look at the prospectus. We need to know which day enrolment starts,' she said, pouring boiling water over the teabags. 'I sent for the prospectus in the first place to find out about the art classes,' she continued. 'I've been intending to take it up again since I left college all those years ago, but I never got round to it.'

She frowned, knowing that after Mike died her enthusiasm had waned and once she'd started to come to terms with losing him, painting just didn't seem to be a priority. But, not wanting to pass on her feelings to Josh, she gave herself a mental shake and lightened up.

'I'll go with you. I'd like a daytime class,' she added. 'I haven't put brush to canvass for years. But I'll give it a go.'

'You ought to do that. Give yourself a break, Mum. You work too hard.'

'It's only three days a week, Josh. I wouldn't want more. I enjoy *Images* and if I could enrol on an art course, I'd be hugely satisfied.

'It says Tuesday and Wednesday next week. What's best for you, Mum?'

'How about Tuesday?'

On Tuesday morning the college was milling with students. Carol and Josh joined the queue and eventually met the tutor for the course Josh had chosen.

'It seems you only just missed out, Josh. I'm willing to accept you provided you agree to attend an evening class for the maths alongside the full time day course.'

Josh looked at Carol, the corners of his mouth curving into a smile. 'Brill,' he said and turning to the tutor added, 'I can do it, sir. Thanks for giving me a chance.'

'That's settled then. Here's a list of the books you'll need. I'll see you Monday.'

Carol and Josh beamed at one another and left the building. Josh, apprehensive after failing his maths, was overjoyed he'd been accepted. That was a pretty good start as far as Carol was concerned.

At the car park Carol opened the car doors and was about to get into the driving seat when Josh intervened.

'Hey Mum. What about your art class?'

'Oh, goodness we were so carried away getting you organised, I clean forgot.'

'Let's get you sorted, Mum,' he said, his confidence now soaring. Taking hold of her elbow, he led her out of the car park as though she was the child and once in the hall, he steered her towards the enrolment desk.

'I'm interested in the Tuesday afternoon watercolour class,' Carol said, smiling.

The woman flicked through the pages of a course reference manual, moved over to the computer and consulted the screen.

'It's full,' she claimed officiously, seemingly with triumph.

Carol was disappointed. 'Is there another day class?'

'There's Thursday afternoon,' the woman offered. 'But you'll have to make it snappy. Painting's been popular this year. There are only two places left.'

Carol was put on the spot. She had expected to join the Tuesday class, but what was the difference between Tuesday or Thursday?

'That's fine. I'd like to join that one, please,' she concluded. 'Is there a list of what's required, the brushes and paints I might need? I'm not familiar with watercolour painting.'

'I'm no expert on painting,' the woman said, her face deadpan. 'You'll have to ask the tutor about that when you get to the class.'

By Monday, Josh had managed to get hold of the text books he needed and Carol had the feeling he was quite looking forward to the course. That was more than she could say for herself. She was beginning to wonder if it had been a mistake enrolling for something she hadn't done since she was in her late teens.

Josh returned on Monday evening, elated. 'Guess what. Will King's on the same course as me.'

'You see. Didn't I tell you it would all work out?' she said, relief surging through her.

'We've decided to study together. It makes sense, Mum,' he added excitedly.

That was the one obstacle over. All she wanted was for Josh to be happy. She felt she owed it to him. He was so unselfish and thoughtful. In fact she wished sometimes he would rebel like some of her friends' teenage sons and daughters. It would make it so much easier for her to let go when the time came.

Thursday came around. She'd finished her work and logged off by midday. After a light lunch she picked up her bag and set off to the college.

There were about a dozen students in the classroom when she arrived, mostly her age or older. That was reassuring. She relaxed.

One of them turned to Carol. 'Hello. I'm Kim. Is this your first year?'

'It is,' she replied. 'By the way, I'm Carol. I haven't painted for almost twenty years, and that was in oils. Watercolour's new to me. I'm terribly out of practice.'

'Don't worry. You'll be fine,' Kim assured her. 'No-one here's an expert. And Katie's really good at bringing out the best in everyone. She's so laid back,' she added.

'That's a relief,' Carol replied, her gaze going to the door as it swung open.

It was the shock of seeing him that caused her heart to shudder in her chest. She could hardly believe her eyes. It was *him*, none other than Paul Trent.

Vibrantly conscious of his physical presence, hot blood rushed to her face. This was incredible. She couldn't believe it possible. To meet someone all those miles away in a foreign country, and then to bump into him again a couple of weeks later was uncanny. Surely it was more than sheer chance?

'I'm your tutor, Paul, Katie's replacement until she's back,' he said, appearing to avoid eye contact with Carol. 'Anyone worked in watercolours before?'

Everyone except Carol raised a hand,

but Paul appeared not to notice her.

With a sudden transition from her dreamy state she re-focused her attention, realising she was the novice. Her stomach churned.

But it wasn't some romantic liaison. She was there to learn, so did it matter that she wasn't up to scratch?

Kim nudged her and whispered, 'I'd clean forgotten. Katie's on maternity leave. I don't know when the baby's due, but she won't be back until January. I think the new tutor's temporary, just filling in.'

'Gather round and I'll explain what I'd like you to do,' Paul said, still showing no sign of recognition towards Carol. He picked up a pencil. 'I'd like us to start with a sketch and then I'll take you through each step of the painting in stages.'

Disappointed that he hadn't even had the manners to acknowledge her, Carol felt foolish and a little edgy too. What had she done to deserve that sort of treatment? She frowned.

Paul's first demonstration turned out to be straightforward. He drew a seascape. Carol had always been good at sketching, it came naturally to her. But when Paul began to demonstrate painting techniques, she started to lose confidence. It wasn't at all like painting in oils, and although the watercolour paints she'd bought were fine, her brushes were totally unsuitable. She took a closer look at them and realised she'd inadvertently picked up the wrong ones in the shop.

Obviously aware that Carol was having problems, Kim nudged her and passed over two brushes. 'Here use these until you get the right ones,' she suggested.

'Thanks, Kim. I'll make sure I change these by next week,' she promised, a feeling of inadequacy building up inside. And as for the actual painting, she knew she needed help, but she was too proud to ask Paul when he'd purposely ignored her.

What was wrong with him? When

they'd parted in France, he'd told her he'd like to have spent more time with her.

It was when Paul approached Kim that Carol became even more rattled. 'Why have you put so much water on your paper?' he asked Kim.

'We always did that with Katie,' Kim replied. 'And then we dropped the paint in afterwards.' She took on a rebellious tone and added, 'I think that's the best way.'

'You do? I see,' he said. 'If that's your technique, then a little less water would be better,' he continued, his lively voice veiling his annoyance. Kim looked embarrassed.

On impulse, Carol gave Paul a long, hard stare as a sudden anger, born of her resentment at his dismissive attitude towards her, his criticism aimed at Kim, flared up inside her.

In return Paul's angry eyes raked her, eyes to intensely blue they seemed to assume a hard sheen. He stepped closer, and his movement appeared intimidating, overpowering, even but she took a deep breath and stood her ground, resisting the urge to back away.

But then his face relaxed, his gaze softened and a smile twitched at the corners of his mouth.

'We seem to have got off on the wrong foot,' he said, obviously trying to diffuse the tensions. 'Let's start with the ground rules. Some of you have been painting for a year or two and already have experience. If you'd prefer to do your own thing, fair enough. But I need to know, and I'm still here to help if you need me.' He paused. 'For those who feel they'd prefer some tuition, I'd like you to follow my instructions,' he added, his tone conciliatory as he moved to the front of the classroom. His anger had now dispersed and his tone was much gentler. 'Any questions?'

No-one spoke. And now Carol felt deflated. He was obviously a man filled with passion and sensitivity about his work and she was aware she had misjudged him.

But Kim interrupted her thoughts. 'Stick with us, Carol,' she whispered under her breath. 'Who does he think he is anyway? We've been coming here for years? I won't be put in my place by the likes of him.' She stared hard at him. 'But he's dishy, I'll give him that.'

Carol was puzzled. What was the point Kim coming to class if she wanted to do her own thing? And she had been tactless when she'd insisted Katie's method was best.

Carol chastised herself severely for the way she'd reacted. Had she not been so frustrated when he'd failed to acknowledge her, perhaps she would have kept out of it.

Paul's voice brought her back sharply. She looked up, instantly aware he was beside her, his eyes watching her with an expression she couldn't define. He smiled.

'You can draw, Carol, I'll give you that. I like the composition, the boat and the children playing on the beach,' he said, his wonderful eyes now gazing with tenderness into hers. 'Just a little more practice with the painting techniques.' He bent down and looked more closely. 'Glad you're here,' he whispered. 'Nice seeing you again.' He moved away.

Unnerved by his closeness, she knew the pull between them was powerful and she needed space and solitude to dream away her thoughts. But this was neither the place nor the time to romanticise. And did she want another man in her life? But where was his wife when he was holidaying in France? That was the mystery.

Despite the disappointing start, the afternoon was a success and, during the remainder of the time in class, she improved her skills tremendously. And now to her surprise he favoured her with the occasional smile.

But why couldn't he have done that in the first place? If he thought he could turn it on and off like that, he could think again.

When the class was over, Carol collected her things, handed the brushes back to Kim and thanked her.

Still puzzled as to why she'd had no sign of recognition from Paul during the early part of the class, Carol tried to convince herself that what she'd felt for him when they were in France had been nothing but a crush, primarily born of his flattering comments. And there was no way she was going to challenge him as to why he'd ignored her.

She was about to leave the room when he called her back. 'Carol. Have you a minute?' One look from those powerful blue eyes and she fell under his spell once again.

Feeling foolish at the way she'd earlier reacted, his words evoked a wry smile. 'Sorry I was uppity,' she said. 'But you didn't even acknowledge me.'

'I suppose it was my fault. But I was stepping into someone else's shoes at very short notice. I had heard Katie was very popular with the students and, even though they're not youngsters, sometimes they resent anyone new. I've gone through it many times before. You see, Carol, I have to establish my stance.'

'How does that affect our friendship?'

'I had no idea you were new to the class. I assumed you were one of them, and I wanted to test the water before I became overly friendly. In the circumstances it was probably the best thing to do, especially when they didn't know you either. They'd have thought we were in cahoots. There's often an adverse reaction, like with Kim, but that's the chance you have to take,' he stressed.

'You've got to agree they were an awkward lot to start with.' He laughed. 'But it was nothing I couldn't handle. Look, let's start fresh,' he said and smiled. 'I was amazed when I walked in and saw you. I just couldn't believe my eyes. I knew you were from the north, but I'd no idea you came from these parts. And to think we have the same interests. That you paint too.'

He slipped a sheet of paper from his case. 'But let's get serious. First of all you need the right equipment. I noticed some of your brushes are actually for use with acrylics. Here I'll give you a list of those you need. These three to start,' he said, pointing them out. 'They are quite expensive, but perhaps you could build up your equipment gradually.'

'Thanks, Paul' she said, grateful they had now ironed out any differences. 'I must confess I realised when I took them out in class that I'd picked up the wrong brushes at the shop. And with nobody to set me on the right path, I came with little knowledge of watercolours. But I'll do as you say, buy just the main ones for now.'

'By the way, despite your lack of experience in watercolour, you're showing quite a talent. Give me a chance to help and we'll soon have you exhibiting.'

Carol was amazed at his words. 'You've got to be joking,' she said. 'I'm a complete beginner, a novice at watercolour. I always worked in oils at college.'

'Don't worry. We'll soon have you up to standard.'

Her face was aglow with excitement but, embarrassed, she laughed and said, 'Thanks for that, Paul. See you next week.' She picked up her bag from the desk.

Changing to pedantic mode, he continued. 'Not so fast, madam.'

Startled she turned to look at him.

'How about a meal at Bellini's in the city on Saturday night? As a peace offering. Can you manage it?'

'I don't know, Paul. I usually cook for Josh in the evenings.'

'Surely for once you could prepare something in advance,' he urged, 'that's what I do for Tom, especially now he's almost eighteen.'

Carol desperately wanted to take up the invitation, but she was playing with fire? After the way things had gone she didn't want him to think she was overly eager.

This was a difficult one to get out of if, in fact, she did want to get out of it.

And she didn't know how Josh might take it, her going off for a meal with Paul. But surely he would have to realise she couldn't spend the rest of her life wondering what he might think. After all, Paul had said it was merely a peace offering.

The debate went on in her mind but, realising he was standing there patiently waiting for a reply, she persuaded herself that she should accept his invitation.

'How can I refuse?' she said, her heart skipping in her chest. 'If it's OK for Tom, it's got to be OK for Josh too. I'll meet you down there at the City Square car park if that's all right with you, Paul,' she added, feeling it was not the right time for Paul to be calling at the house.

'That's fine by me, but I'd willingly pick you up,' he told her.

'Thanks, but I'm not sure what the arrangements will be with Josh. He may need a lift somewhere before I meet you.'

'I see,' Paul conceded. 'Then I look forward to Saturday.'

Despite her elation that Paul had entered her life again, her confidence waned when it was time to tell Josh about the invitation. Maybe it was her conscience. But why should she feel guilty? It was eight years since she'd lost Mike and her precious memories were locked away never to be forgotten.

Surely she deserved another shot at happiness. She strengthened her resolve. It was a friendship, nothing more.

But the minute she broached the subject with Josh she knew by the look on his face he felt some sort of discomfort.

'I must say, Mum, it doesn't take you long to get in with the staff,' he joked, intimating he was making light of the issue, but Carol knew differently.

'But I told you, Josh. It's Paul Trent I'm meeting, Tom's dad.'

'Does that make a difference?' he asked.

'Of course it does. We were already friends before I went to college.'

'Where exactly are you going?' Josh asked, his face taking on a serious look.

Determined not to let Josh dictate, or try to get the better of her, she said quite openly, 'Bellini's, that lovely Italian restaurant in the city. Surely you don't begrudge me a night out for a change?' Now she was the one who threw out the challenge.

Either she'd touched a nerve or he felt sheepish that he'd questioned her so rigidly. His frown turned to a smile.

'Of course, I don't,' he said. 'I was only kidding. You go, Mum and enjoy it. You never go anywhere these days. In any case, Will and I are going bowling. He's getting a take-away from the Indian. I could do the same if you like.'

'Good idea,' she said, inwardly sighing with relief. It was obvious Josh had been stunned at first but, now that his own social life was extending, he would have to realise his mother needed more in her life than work and domestic chores, all of which kept her in the house for most of the day.

He gave a little smirk. 'And behave yourself,' he said pointing a finger as though reprimanding her, at the same time dodging the playful flick of her hand, 'or you'll have me to answer to!'

Carol laughed. 'You're getting a bit too cheeky since you started that college course,' she said. 'Don't forget who the boss is.'

'I won't,' he said, pulling himself up to his full height. Now he was taking on the dominant male role. But at least he was laughing which meant he wasn't as uptight about her date with Paul as she'd expected.

3

Not wanting to appear too flamboyant, Carol chose a little cream suit that was plain but figure-hugging, one she'd worn earlier in the year at her interview with Barron and Weeks. Her heart fluttered as she drove towards the car park in City Square.

Paul was there waiting, and she was drawn by his sheer physical magnetism. He had that in abundance.

'Hi,' he called out, positively grinning, pleasure sparkling in his eyes. Taking her hand in his, he scanned her from head to toe and added, 'You look wonderful.'

Carol stared back wide-eyed as she tried to absorb the impact of meeting up with him again.

'Done your homework?' he joked.

'Haven't had time for that,' she said, smiling up at him, 'But don't worry. I'll do it before next Thursday.'

'Can't put you in for the Turner Prize if you don't get on with it,' he added, a smile twitching at the corners of his mouth.

They both laughed, and it seemed they had overcome any embarrassment.

He took her arm and led her across the busy road. She felt the closeness of his body next to hers and when she glanced sideways she noticed a devastating smile dancing around his mouth. He caught her gaze and his eyes reflected a faint trace of amusement. And he didn't let go when they reached the far side of the road. He clasped her hand firmly and tucked it under his arm. She shuddered.

'By the way,' he said, 'I meant to ask you how things went for Josh at school?'

'He didn't go back to school,' she told him. 'He decided on college instead. They're far more accommodating. Josh seems to be enjoying it tremendously.'

'That's good,' Paul replied. 'I must

look out for him.'

'How about Tom? He's at university now, I take it.'

'Yes. I'm talking to myself at home. But seriously, I do miss him,' he said wistfully.

Carol detected a vague sadness to his voice, and it seemed to her it concerned much more than Tom going to university. She was puzzled. Paul had asked her out and by now she'd assumed he had no partner. But the same question kept bombarding her mind. Was he a widower or maybe a divorcee? He didn't seem ready to tell her.

Not yet. And she wasn't going to ask.

They entered the restaurant and Carol was surprised to see so many people in there. The waiter ushered them through to one of the tables at the back of the restaurant.

'I especially asked for a table here,' Paul explained, taking her coat. 'I find it difficult trying to compete with all that noise.'

Carol nodded and smile. 'I'm not surprised.'

'Drinks?' The waiter took her coat and hovered.

'I'd like a white wine spritzer, please,' Carol replied.

'One for me too, waiter,' Paul echoed. He handed Carol a menu. 'Now, how about a starter? What will you have?'

She ran her finger down the menu. 'I can't resist the scallops au gratin,' she confessed as she looked up at him. Her stomach gave a tiny shimmer. He was doing it again, giving her that look.

'That's settled then. I rather fancy the moules mariniere. How about pizza and salad for mains?'

'If I can manage it,' she said. 'But you choose the pizza. Any would suit me.'

'Good. That's settled then,' he said as the waiter arrived with the drinks.

Paul lifted his glass. 'Here's to good times ahead and success with the painting.'

'Cheers,' she echoed, taking a sip.

Myriad thoughts chased through her mind. But after a few seconds she broke the silence. 'I'm very impressed by your painting. I take it you're an artist by profession.'

'That's right. I do a little tutoring to keep my hand in, but only on a temporary basis. Once the famous Katie returns to the college I'm let off the hook.'

'How many classes do you have?'

'Just a couple, the one you attend and another across the city. I spend most of my time in the studio at home.'

'I work from home too, for Barron and Weeks, processing house conveyances. But it can be a rather lonely existence.'

'I didn't realise you were in the same boat. At least you have the class on Thursday to get you out.'

'I go to *Images* too. It's the local health club. I enjoy that.'

'And it keeps you in shape,' he said, a grin sketching his face. 'I'm afraid I have a problem sparing the time for anything like that. But I always take time off to be with Tom in the school holidays.'

'Going back to the painting, what's your favourite medium, Paul?'

'I use watercolour, acrylic and oil, sometimes individually and sometimes mixed. My agent researches the market and tells me what's in vogue. I particularly enjoyed working outdoors when we were on holiday.'

'You paint on holiday, too? I didn't realise that.' Now his days away when they were in France made sense. He was out painting.

'Tom paints too. He's a talented artist, but we're completely different in style. He enjoys the surrealist approach, but that's not for me.'

'Nor me. I suppose my style is rather passe.'

'Don't say that, Carol. It's a matter of taste, especially when it comes to public demand,' he was keen to point out.

Carol was beginning to enjoy their discussion. Art had been one of her passions all those years ago. It was coming back to her now and she became engrossed.

Eventually the conversation turned to Josh. 'I take it Josh was OK about your leaving him to get his own meal,' Paul said.

'A little prickly at first, not about being left, more that I was going out with someone. He's not used to anyone else entering our cosy little duo. And he can be quite shy at times. Once he gains a little confidence and gets to know someone, he's fine. He's very much like his father.

'I take it you're not together — you and your husband.'

Carol looked away momentarily. 'He was killed in a car crash when Josh was seven. We miss him terribly.'

'I'm so sorry, Carol. I didn't mean to pry.'

'Don't worry, Paul. It's taken years to get over losing him. The memories never leave you. But life must go on.'

'I couldn't agree more.'

His eyes became livelier and he switched the topic. 'About you. Any other hobbies?'

'I've no time left after the health club and now the art class.'

The waiter appeared with the starters.

'These scallops look delicious with the cheese sauce topping.' Carol took one from the shell. 'This is delightful,' she said.

'Mine too. I haven't had moules in ages and these are particularly good.'

When the main course arrived, Carol knew she could tackle the salad, but only a small portion of pizza. She struggled and eventually had to give in.

'I couldn't eat another thing,' she confessed, leaning back in her chair.

'All the more for me,' Paul said, winking roguishly.

Her heart fluttered in her chest. 'It's been good, Paul. I haven't enjoyed myself so much in ages.'

'Nor me.' He slipped his hand across the table to cover hers, a puzzled look on his face. 'I'm amazed you've not remarried. With your looks and dare I say, a very attractive figure, you must have had your fair share of admirers.'

'I've been so wrapped up caring for Josh single-handed, I've had neither the time nor the inclination. You're the only man I've been out with since Mike, apart from close friends and relatives.'

'I'm surprised at that. I'll give you full marks for loyalty. But you can't hold on to your memories forever to the exclusion of everything else. Everyone deserves some happiness.' He sighed. 'But I'm glad we've cleared the air after that disastrous start at the college.'

Carol laughed. 'And I didn't help,' she relied, 'giving you my frosty look. But it was partly your fault,' she joked.

'I know. Don't remind me,' he said grinning. 'But it's all in the past. Forget it. We must do this again,' he urged.

'I'd like that. We have a common interest.'

'Good,' he said, looking at his watch. 'Sorry to have to break up the party. I need to get back now. I'm expecting an important phone call at ten from my agent. He knew I'd be out earlier.'

He took her jacket, slipped it around her, lifted her silky hair and gripped her shoulders. 'I hope you don't feel I'm pushing you off. It's been great spending time with you.'

She felt the warmth of his breath on the back of her neck and she felt her concentration lapse. It was unsettling and she felt an overwhelming temptation to turn and snuggle into his arms.

'I must get back too, Paul. It won't be long before I'm in bed tonight. I've a mound of work to do tomorrow. And I need to be back for Josh, make sure he doesn't stay out too late.'

After paying the bill they left Bellini's and strolled back to the car park. 'Take care going back. I'll see you on Thursday.'

Paul stared hard into her eyes and gently placed his arms around her, drawing him to her. She felt her body relax as she leant against his chest, feeling safe in the comforting warmth of his strong arms. Then he released her slightly and kissed her on both cheeks.

'Just a parting gesture,' he joked, his eyes simmering with more than casual warmth, setting her heart thumping again.

Carol stepped into her car and left, butterflies still dancing around in her stomach as she drove home. That feeling of closeness came over her again and again and she tried to brush it away. But it was difficult.

What a magical evening, easy conversation with Paul and utterly relaxing. But what did she know about him? Very little. Once more she'd rambled on about her own circumstances and Paul had offered virtually nothing.

* * *

He was warmer towards her in class, but he obviously didn't want to show any favouritism. After an hour, Kim and the others were beginning to settle down and the sniping comments stopped. Kim even started to smile at him, especially when he commented positively on her drawing.

Carol had managed to practise the wet-into-wet techniques over the week-end and when Paul asked the group to paint a Mediterranean sky she was quite pleased with the result. He was too.

'How about painting the seashore using the same principle, but with yellow ochre and a little cadmium?' he suggested. 'When you've finished, make sure you leave it to dry. Whatever you do, don't be tempted to tear it up even if you're not happy with it. There'll be a massive difference when it's dry. The change is remarkable.'

Carol put the Mediterranean scene to one side and started to sketch the gondolas. It took ten minutes to complete and by that time her first picture was dry. Starting on the next stage, she concentrated hard, but before she knew it Paul had asked them to clear away. The class was at an end.

Her stomach plummeted. She wouldn't see him for another week. But she knew she shouldn't be thinking like that and she chastised herself severely.

She tried telling herself *she* wasn't looking for a relationship either. But there was no harm in another meal together, just as friends. He was the one who'd suggested they do it again some time.

'Don't forget, plenty of practice before next week,' he called after her.

'I'll try my best,' she said and she left the college with an empty feeling inside.

Josh and Will were there revising maths when she returned home. 'This is sinking in much better now that we've gone over it again with Mr Wallis. He's really good isn't he, Will?'

'I'll say. Better than Ma Scott as school,' Will replied and they both smirked.

'I'm glad you're enjoying it,' Carol said.

'How did your class go, Mum?' Josh asked her.

'Fine. I'm getting into it now.'

'Let's have a look at what you did today.'

'They're nothing special,' she said, wishing Josh hadn't asked her. But she slid the partially-completed pictures from her case and passed them over.

Josh took hold of them. 'Wow, they're brill. These are wicked, Mum.'

'They're not that good,' Carol said modestly. 'But all the same I'm pleased with them,' she added and she slipped the pictures back into her case.

Quickly changing the subject, she said, 'I'll start making the meal. Would you like to stay, Will?'

'Thanks Mrs Henderson, but Mum's expecting me back at six o'clock.'

Josh chipped in. 'Will and I were thinking of taking a couple of hours off tonight. There's a good film on at Unit Four.'

'Fine, Josh, but in that case I'll leave my meal until later. I'll pop down to the club, do my usual circuit and take a swim. I'll eat when I come back.'

After he'd eaten, Josh left as Carol

collected her sports bag and set off for *Images*. It was the twilight hour when most people were returning from work.

The gym was almost empty when she arrived. That was how she liked it in the evenings, relatively quiet with the freedom to choose her equipment.

Slipping her earphones from the sports bag, she plugged them into one of the music channels on the treadmill.

But midway through her session she was distracted by a man who had started up the treadmill next to hers. Instead of power-walking, he began to run quite fast. And then out of the corner of her eye, Carol was aware he had adjusted the incline on the machine. Now he was running uphill.

He turned and smiled. Carol quickly looked away, a hot flush spreading from her chin to her forehead, a reaction she didn't want. But she was being rude. She turned back, and giving him a weak half smile, she sincerely hoped he didn't think she was giving him the come-on.

Determined to take control, she took

a deep breath and reverted to the present. The man next to her smiled once more and she reciprocated. She couldn't very well ignore him.

Her programme complete, she decided to take a sauna.

It was so hot Carol could barely withstand the heat and after five minutes she came out, took a cold shower and made for the steam room, hoping it wouldn't be as hot in there. She sat down and peered through the steam, realising there was someone else sitting on the bench opposite her.

'Hello again.' It was a male voice.

'Hello,' she said straining to see through half-closed eyes. And then she recognised the dark-haired man, the one who'd been on the treadmill next to her.

'I need to relax,' he said. 'The treadmill is a real challenge.'

'I'm not surprised you need to relax. That was some pace you were doing, and quite an incline too. I must say you seem to enjoy punishing yourself.' Carol smiled.

'You didn't do so badly yourself,' he said. 'Have you been coming here long?'

'Since the club opened. It's an absolute boon after a day's work.'

'I couldn't agree more. Have you finished for the day?' he asked.

Oh, no, she thought, not wishing to become involved in a trivial conversation. What was it to him whether she'd finished or not?

'I'm hoping to swim,' she told him.

He came towards her and extended his hand. 'Simon Rothwell,' he added. 'And you're . . . '

'Carol Henderson,' she replied a little reluctantly, now standing up and scanning the pool through the glass door. 'I think that'll do.' She reached for the handle. 'I need to get on with my swim. I'll see you around, Simon.'

'Before you rush off, how about a drink in the bar afterwards.'

So that was it. He was chatting her up. 'I'm sorry but I can't, not tonight. I've already been here longer than I'd planned. My son will be expecting me.'

'Maybe some other time,' he added.

'Thanks for asking,' she said politely, secretly heaving a sigh of relief, telling herself she needed to maintain her independence.

Things took an unusual turn on Carol's next visit to the club. After finishing her workout in the gym, she went downstairs to the pool area and set about her kilometre swim.

Now changing from breaststroke to front crawl, her pace was brisk, but by the time she was on her final lap the strain was telling. When she pulled herself out of the water her breathing was heavy.

Feeling satisfied that she'd fulfilled her challenge she made for the steam room and, taking a deep breath to replenish her oxygen level, she pulled open the door and entered. It was empty in there and, stretching out on the bench, she let the steam envelop her. What luxury. She closed her eyes and let herself drift.

When she came round she was being lifted from the bench.

'Don't worry,' came a distant echo.

She was being carried by strong arms out of the steam room. Alarmed, she tried to free herself from the grip, but she had no energy. What was happening to her, and where on earth was she?

'You'll be fine,' the gentle yet familiar voice continued.

When eventually Carol managed to focus her eyes, she realised it was Simon who was carrying her. Beside him was one of the lifeguards, Rick. She felt herself being set down on a soft surface and, when she tried to pull herself up, she felt weak.

'What happened?' she whispered.

'You passed out,' Rick told her. 'It was lucky Simon found you. I'd looked in the steam room myself just before you left the pool. You can't have been in there more than a couple of minutes before Simon joined you.'

'I'm sorry if I've been a nuisance,' Carol said, closing her eyes and trying to shake herself into full control. 'I felt so relaxed.'

'A little too relaxed,' Simon insisted. 'You didn't answer me when I spoke to you. That's why I knew something was wrong.'

'I saw you swimming,' Rick told her, 'and I was impressed. You must have done those last few laps in record time. But you should have taken a few minutes' rest before you went into the steam room.'

'You're OK now.' Simon laughed. 'Don't worry. I know what it's like. We're as bad as each other trying to hang on to our youth,' he added, trying to make light of the situation. 'We think we're still teenagers. I'm as much a culprit as you are. But on this occasion you overdid it.'

'But I've never passed out in my life,' Carol stressed. 'Why now?'

'It was just one of those things,' Rick told her. 'And the steam room was particularly hot today. Just remember to take a rest in the future.'

Carol felt hugely embarrassed. What must they be thinking? That she was some sort of wimp. And to be carried out of the steam room in front of the other swimmers! How would she ever face anyone at the club again?

But, not wanting to make an issue, she pulled herself up from the bench and said jokingly, 'I suppose some people will do anything for attention.' The other two laughed.

And them Simon spoke. 'You can't refuse me this time,' he insisted. 'You need to relax and have a warm drink, just until you feel ready to leave. I suggest you go and change. Meet me at the café. I know you may think you feel OK, but it would be sensible to do as I say.'

'You're not going to give in are you?' she said, smiling back at Simon. He was certainly in his element issuing orders. But she knew he was only being kind and caring after what had happened. 'I'm fine. You don't have to worry any more.'

'Maybe not, but I'm not going to let you drive home until you've had a drink with plenty of sugar to sustain your energy level.'

She showered and dressed, collected her things from the locker and went through to the café area where Simon was waiting for her.

'Come and sit down,' he said, patting the seat beside him. 'What will you have?'

'I'd love a cappuccino,' she replied. 'That should revive me.' She sat down. 'But I feel such an idiot.'

'The pool was almost empty when we brought you out of the steam room, maybe a couple of swimmers, but no more. So don't worry about it. As I said earlier, it's just one of those things. It could have happened to any of us.'

They made light conversation and Carol discovered that Simon was the managing director of a leisurewear manufacturing company, hence his keenness on keeping fit.

'I must keep up the image,' he told

her, grinning youthfully. 'I make it company policy to encourage both my executive and sales staff to attend a sports centre. Most do, but some have slackened off recently. I tend to give a few hints in the hope they'll resume the programme.'

'You're quite a taskmaster,' Carol joked. 'I wouldn't like to be in their shoes. What's the name of the company?'

Simon paused. 'It's called *Fast Gear*,' he said. 'But it's not in this area.

'You must have quite a distance to travel.'

'It's not all that far, just south of Sheffield,' he said.

She drained her coffee cup and stood up to leave. 'Thanks again, Simon. I really am grateful for your help.'

'It's the least I could do, Carol,' he replied and then he added, 'You mentioned you had a son. Are there just the two of you?'

'Yes, and that's how we like it. No complications,' she chuckled.

'I'm divorced too,' he offered, looking

up at her and obviously believing they were two of a kind. 'But we don't want to go into that,' he added with finality.

Carol didn't put him straight about her own circumstances. There was no point. She didn't owe anyone an explanation.

4

It was a few days after the incident when Carol bumped into Simon again at the club.

'Hi, Carol,' he called across the empty gym. 'How are you feeling?'

'I'm fine now,' she replied as he came towards her. 'I'm sure it was nothing but a blip. I overstepped the mark. But I've learned my lesson, thanks to you.'

After ten minutes on the treadmill Carol moved to the rowing machine. Simon followed and set off running on the treadmill.

'I have two tickets to see *Mama Mia* at the Royal on Friday night. Do you fancy coming along?' he asked casually. He smiled. 'And before you decide, it's purely platonic, I promise.'

Initially she was reluctant to make arrangements. She barely knew him and, in any case, there was a genuine reason why she couldn't take up the offer.

'Sorry I can't manage Friday, Simon. Josh and I are going to a family party. But it does sound tempting. It's the Abba musical isn't it?'

'Yes it is. That's a pity,' he said momentarily. 'But maybe I could exchange the tickets for Saturday. Would you be free then? It might be fully booked, but I have a good contact. I may be able to pull a few strings,' He grinned.

'As far as I can recall, yes I am free,' she offered, now taken off her guard.

'Then how about it?'

She made a snap decision. He had given her the 'no strings attached' promise, and his word was good enough for her. 'I'd like that,' she said.

'Are you here tomorrow afternoon?'

'Not until after four.'

'I'll check it out and see you then. We could go to La Rue afterwards. I've not been before, but I've heard the food there is excellent, and I'd like to try it out.'

'Sounds good,' she said, still wondering if she'd made the right decision.

When Simon told her he'd managed to change the tickets and book the restaurant for the Saturday evening, Carol had a feeling of warmth inside. It was good to be asked out again. And it was certainly a record, two invites within the space of a couple of weeks.

But something nagged away inside her. She couldn't help wishing the invite had come from Paul.

★   ★   ★

Thursday came around and there was a buzz in the art room. After the shaky start to the course the students now freely admitted how much they enjoyed Paul's tuition. Their respect for him had grown. But Katie was due back some time in January, and they were aware that Paul wouldn't be with them much longer.

As soon as he entered the room he hushed the group.

'There's something I'd like to run by you, something I've been contemplating for a day or two.' He sat down. 'I've been so impressed with the progress you've made that, before I leave, I'd like us to stage an exhibition, show the public the quality of your work. I've discussed my plan with the principal and she's in favour,' he said.

'There's a rich variety of talent within the group. You all have your own strengths and styles, and a whole host of genres — landscapes, flowers, animals, portraits. An exhibition would show the versatility of the group. What do you think?'

'I for one couldn't produce anything good enough for an exhibition, Paul,' Kim said, folding her arms and frowning.

'Nonsense,' Paul continued. 'How about the landscape you finished last week? I'd like something from you all. Now do I have your agreement?' he urged as he gazed at the uncertain looks on the faces of some of the students.

'Trust me your work is more than adequate for a student exhibition. You're one of the best groups I've taught in a long time. Be confident. You know you can do it,' he stressed and he laughed. 'Show of hands, please.'

One or two of the students put up their hands and gradually the others followed suit.

'What about mounting and framing the pictures?' Kim asked.

'I'll arrange to have them done at cost. It won't be much. I'll discuss your work individually, give you an idea what would be best for you to submit.'

Excitement flared throughout the room, but at this point, like Kim, Carol began to have doubts about the standard of her work. Surely he didn't expect her to contribute after only a few months in the class.

When he approached her to discuss her work she told him of her fears. 'I've not had as much experience in watercolour as the others. Maybe next time.'

'Nonsense. You're as good if not better than most,' he stressed in hushed tones. 'You already have two or three pictures in your portfolio I'd like you to submit.'

'Oh I don't know, Paul.' Carol bit her lip.

'Well I do. Decision made,' he concluded.

Despite her fears, Carol was delighted that Paul had included her and, at the end of the class, he asked her to stay back for a few minutes.

'Go for it, Carol. I can't tell you enough how good your work is. Now to change the subject, I thought maybe we could go out for a bite to eat on Saturday night if you're free.' His blue eyes rested on hers, a look of anticipation sketching his face.

Carol's stomach gave a little flurry. She felt bad knowing she would have to turn him down. 'I'm sorry Paul, but I've already made arrangements for Saturday. Maybe some time next week,' she suggested.

'It's difficult for me to make spontaneous arrangements at the moment,' he said, a frown sketching his face. 'I've been commissioned to paint a set of family portraits in oils, and I need to stick to my arrangements. Don't worry. I knew it was rather short notice. But I thought it was worth a try.'

Carol's first reaction was one of disappointment that she'd made arrangements with Simon. But she realised that was unkind of her.

They got on well together and, after all, he'd been very thoughtful and caring towards her. In any case, maybe she would have appeared overly eager had she agreed to meet Paul at such short notice.

It was six-thirty on Saturday by the time Paul had completed Gloria Peel's portrait. With an anxious look on her face, Gloria moved towards the easel, taking a first furtive glance at the canvass. Her eyes opened wide in surprise.

'My goodness,' she said, obviously

taken aback at the likeness. 'It's wonderful, Paul. I'm thrilled to bits.'

She slipped her arms into her camel coat and collected her handbag from the chair. 'George will be here tomorrow afternoon. You must be firm and make him stay put. He hasn't an ounce of patience. He'll be fidgeting all the time.'

Paul laughed. 'Then maybe it would be better if we did the portrait in easy stages, perhaps in two or three sessions. I'd prefer that rather than have him scowling at me all afternoon,' he said laughing.

'Good idea, Paul. I'm sure he'd be delighted at that.'

The mill on the outskirts of the village had belonged to the Peel family for several generations, and it was customary for the portraits of the directors to be hung in the huge reception area.

When Paul was a boy his father had been commissioned to paint the portraits of the previous generation, but now George and his wife, Gloria, had taken over. Paul was proud to carry on the tradition.

He left the house and headed for the Prachee Restaurant in the city centre hoping it wouldn't be too crowded. Granted it was Saturday night, but surely they'd have room somewhere in the restaurant for a single diner.

It was a few minutes before he found a parking space. He placed the ticket on the dashboard, locked up and headed towards City Square and the restaurant. The traffic was heavy and he dodged between the stationary cars waiting at the lights. It was then he saw a familiar face.

Stunned, he turned to take a second look. There was no mistaking it was Carol. She was languishing in the passenger seat of a BMW sports car and, as Paul peered more closely, he realised the driver was a man about his own age.

That was strange. Carol had told him she hadn't been out with anyone since her husband had died, yet here she was with this guy in an expensive sports car. To be fair, she had told him she wasn't available Saturday night, and whoever she chose to go out with was none of his business.

But deep down he had a feeling of unease. His heart flipped in his chest and he confessed to himself that he was jealous.

When the lights changed to green and the traffic started to move Carol was laughing as she turned to look out of the car window. Paul quickly looked away. The last thing he wanted was for her to see him there staring.

The meal at the Prachee was enjoyable, but he felt lonely. Conversation was part of the social occasion and it was at times like these when he missed Tom.

Thinking about Tom triggered thoughts of Diane. He hadn't been to see her for two days and he must visit on Sunday. George would be sitting for the portrait during the afternoon. It would have to be the evening.

He had hoped to telephone Carol and ask her out Sunday evening, but now that he'd seen her with the guy in the sports car, he felt it would be better to leave the invite until the following week.

If he was a new man in her life, perhaps he should given them plenty of leeway. He didn't want to cramp their style.

Carol had been surprised to see the sleek silver sports car parked outside. She smiled to herself.

The green silk dress she'd chosen to wear was one of her own creations. It was plain but slinky and, to give the understated effect, she decided not to wear jewellery.

Outside, the car door stood open for her. Simon, immaculate in a dark lounge suit, held her hand as she slid into the seat. They left for the theatre and Carol realised this was an experience with a difference. It was good to be pampered.

Throughout the journey their conversation was light. Carol felt completely at ease with Simon and, to her surprise, they seemed to have so much in common.

The performance was about to start as they took their seats. 'Just in time,' Simon whispered.

Carol became engrossed in the show, and at the end she applauded with vigour. 'That was brilliant, Simon. I wouldn't have missed it for the world. Thanks for bringing me.'

They laughed together as Simon led her from the theatre back to the car park and when he closed the passenger door behind her, Carol took a furtive glance at her watch. It was already nine-thirty, quite late to be starting a meal and, although Josh had gone out with Will, she knew he would be back by eleven.

However, there was nothing she could do about it. She'd agreed to Simon booking the meal at the French bistro in the first place, but she was surprised when they left the city and headed for the suburbs. She had expected the restaurant to be close to the theatre.

'It's not far away,' Simon told her as they neared a small village close to the moors, and when they arrived at La Rue they were ushered to a table in an alcove by the window. Simon turned to her and said, 'This is a new experience for me, too. But I've heard the food is wonderful.'

'I'm not surprised you're so harsh with yourself on the treadmill if this is the sort of place you frequent,' she said, smiling and realising it was an expensive restaurant. 'The food here smells delightful.'

'You're right. I manage to keep the weight off by exercising.' He leant on his elbows and continued. 'I enjoy visiting good restaurants, sampling cordon bleu food.' He paused. 'There's another place I'd like to take you. I discovered it quite unexpectedly one night when Julie was away touring. I'd had a particularly stressful day at work and needed to get out of the house and think things through.'

'I take it Julie's your ex-wife.'

'That's right,' Simon confirmed.

'When you say Julie was touring, did you mean on stage?'

'Yes, Julie's an opera singer. She has one heck of a talent. She was invited to tour and, of course, she couldn't resist. Who could blame her? But she was away for weeks at a time and eventually we drifted apart. It was no marriage for either of us.'

'I didn't realise Julie Rothwell was your wife. I've seen her in concert. She's brilliant.'

'Yes, she has a wonderful voice. She made her decision and chose to continue touring. She was as much entitled to a career as I was. We parted amicably and I genuinely wished her every success. A year after we split she phoned and asked for a divorce.'

'But do you have any children?'

'I'm afraid not. In view of Julie's career, we kept on postponing the decision, but that's something I do regret.'

'I suppose there are two ways of looking at it. Children are good company, but a divorce can affect them psychologically. They can easily become confused as to where their allegiances lie, especially when new partners are involved.'

'Yes, it must be hard for youngsters to cope.' He pondered momentarily and the continued. 'How has your son coped?'

For a second or two she didn't see the link, and then she realised what he meant.

'Oh, I'm not divorced, Simon. I'm a widow. Josh did suffer when Mike died, but he lost his father permanently which gave some finality to it. We still have our memories.'

'Do forgive me, Carol. I made an assumption and I shouldn't have.'

'Don't worry about it. You weren't to know.'

Carol changed the subject and they chatted amicably, Simon about his business, Carol about her job with Barron and Weeks.

'You mentioned a college course.

What are you studying?'

'It's nothing academic. It's a leisure course — watercolour painting.'

'Sounds interesting. I wouldn't mind seeing your paintings some time,' he said, and then he started to laugh. 'I'm not propositioning you, honestly. I didn't mean it like that.'

'Of course not. And in any case, I'm not up to standard, not yet.' She giggled. 'Although the tutor has suggested we submit paintings for an exhibition he's setting up.'

'Well then, maybe I'll be allowed to come to the exhibition. How about it?'

'Oh I don't know, Simon. I'm nervous enough about it without my friends coming along,' she said, wishing she hadn't allowed herself to be so flippant and ramble on.

'Don't hide your light under a bushel,' he said. 'You must be good enough or the tutor wouldn't have accepted your work.'

'We'll see,' Carol said, kicking herself for even mentioning the art class. She'd only mentioned the exhibition in fun, not expecting such a reaction.

The meal over, the waiter brought the bill. Simon slipped a credit card on top and handed it straight back, obviously wanting to keep the cost of the meal from her. Not that she would have embarrassed him by taking a sly peek at the bill or offering to pay her share.

Instead she would reciprocate at some future date. When the waiter returned with the slip Simon signed it with a flourish and left the restaurant.

The easy conversation continued on the way back and, once outside her house, he turned and gave her a light peck on the cheek.

'See you at the club,' he said. 'Will you be there tomorrow?'

'I don't go on Sundays when Josh is home. But I'll see you next week,' she said, 'Thanks again Simon. It's been great,' she added as she approached the front door.

★　★　★

After closing it behind her she leant with her back to it mulling over the events of the last couple of weeks. Two delightful evenings in that space of time after all those years staying home and remaining loyal to Mike.

'Come on, Mum. Stop day-dreaming,' came the call from the lounge. Josh came towards her. 'And what time do you call this?' he asked, looking at his watch and smiling.

'Time you were in bed, young man,' she said taking his hand and giving it a squeeze.

'I had to wait up for you, Mum. I needed to know you were back,' he said, a look of genuine concern on his face.

'I know I'm late Josh, but it couldn't be helped. We seemed to go miles to La Rue. But it was worth it. The food was delicious.'

'Glad you enjoyed it, Mum. See you in the morning.'

*   *   *

Carol's four pictures, all loosely painted floral arrangements, were mounted and framed ready for the exhibition. Paul set them out on the desk in front of her.

'There. Didn't I tell you what a difference framing would make?' he said, his eyes alight with pride on her behalf.

'Wow. You're right, Paul,' she said, admitting to herself that the ivory mounts enhanced the pictures and brought out the delicate colours of the flowers. 'I'm absolutely delighted. My confidence is soaring,' she joked, rolling her eyes and laughing.

'Well, they're not quite ready for the Turner Prize yet, but I promise you, some day . . . ' he added, joining in the laughter.

Their hilarity attracted Kim who came across to look. 'They're great, Carol. I can't believe what a difference the mounting and framing makes.'

'I'll say,' Carol agreed, looking at Kim's work. 'Yours are super. The mounting gives them a whole new perspective.

Paul continued, 'Right, listen to me. Rule number one. If we're to be professional in our approach, we need to mark up a realistic price for each picture. Even if it's just a few pounds to cover the materials, at least you'd get back what you've spent on framing. We're nearing Christmas and people often like to buy presents that are different. And these are certainly quality gifts at bargain prices.' Paul was trying to be serious, but his comment caused shrieks of laughter.

'Oh dear,' Kim said, pursing her mouth and pulling a face. 'Mine are so precious, money couldn't buy them.'

'I see you've changed your tune, Kim — *I couldn't possibly produce anything to exhibit*,' he said, mocking her initial reaction playfully. 'I'd like all the exhibits in before Friday,' Paul told them at the end of the class. 'That's the latest I can put them on display for the exhibition on Saturday.'

Carol made no further mention of the exhibition to Simon, hoping he would have forgotten about it. But on the Friday evening he caught up with her at the club.

'I saw the poster advertising the exhibition. Now you can't deny me a peek at your pictures,' he said, slipping his arm around her shoulder in a friendly gesture.

'I must say, you are persistent,' she said, her huge brown eyes sparkling. 'I'll be there Saturday afternoon. If you drop in then, perhaps I could show you round. I'll meet you at the door.'

'It's a deal,' he replied. 'About two,' he added without waiting for a reply.

She must stop this. Now she was becoming over-confident. There must be a happy medium. She pulled her thoughts together. She had a nagging feeling of regret at the back of her mind that she'd allowed Simon to intrude into something that was Paul's sphere. But there was nothing she could do about it now.

On the Saturday afternoon, Carol waited near the main door for Simon.

According to Kim, Paul had been there during the earlier part of the morning, but he'd left just before Carol arrived and no-one seemed to know when he'd be returning in the afternoon.

It was just before two when Simon turned up. 'I can't wait to see these works of art,' he said, rubbing his hands together.

'Now you're making me nervous,' Carol confessed, taking his arm and leading him to the main hall.

As they entered the exhibition Josh and Will approached them.

'Where've you been, Mum? I've looked everywhere for you,' Josh said, a tone of resentment in his voice. 'Anyway, it's good news,' he continued, lightening up.

'I was waiting at the main door,' she said, surprised at the sharpness in his voice. 'What do you mean good news?'

'Guess what! Someone's bought all your pictures. They're still there, but they all have red stickers on them. That does mean someone's bought them, doesn't it?'

'It does, Josh, but surely you've got it wrong.' Carol couldn't believe what she was hearing.

'Give me credit, Mum. I do know which pictures are yours,' he said with finality as he shot a fixed stare at Simon's arm which was now comfortably draped around his mother's shoulders.

Carol noticed the look on his face, but she did nothing about it. 'By the way, this is Simon, one of my friends from *Images*. Simon, meet Josh, and his friend, Will.'

Simon extended his hand. 'Pleased to meet you, Josh. You too, Will. I gather you're studying at the college too.'

'That's right,' Josh replied, a sullen look on his face. He turned to his mother. 'Come on, Mum. Have a look at the pictures. That'll prove I'm right.'

Josh led her to the other side of the hall where her pictures were displayed. Sure enough all four had red stickers on the bottom right hand corners.

'I just can't believe it,' Carol said,

staring in disbelief. 'They've only been here since this morning. Someone must be playing a prank on me,' she added.

'I don't think so,' came a familiar voice from behind.

Carol spun round. It was Paul. 'Hello Paul. Glad you're here. But how do you mean?'

'They were bought by someone I know. He'd like more. But we'll talk it through later,' he said turning and leaving them all with bewildered looks on their faces.

* * *

Paul left the hall and went across the road to his classroom. He'd been elated when Guy Rollinson had bought Carol's pictures, even more so when he'd asked for more.

Guy owned a top-notch gallery in Westerton, a popular tourist town in the Dales. This could be the start of something big if the pictures made the popular market.

But the thrill of excitement was tainted when he spotted that guy with Carol, the one with the expensive sports car.

He opened his briefcase and took out the cheque Guy had left with him that morning, the one written out to Carol. He slipped it into his top pocket and left the room. The best plan was to telephone her the next day, Sunday.

She'd surely be spending Saturday evening with her gentleman friend, especially after the good news.

When he returned to the hall, Carol and her little group had gone. He supposed there was no reason for her to remain there now that her pictures had sold.

He wandered back through the hall and noticed one or two of the pictures had sold, but not on complete sets. He'd kept on telling Carol it wouldn't take long for her to find success, and it had happened in such a short space of time. He felt proud. Could he call her a prodigy of his?

But maybe he was thinking too far ahead. Maybe he should wait and see if she was prepared to take up the commission from Guy.

The exhibition would be closing at four-thirty and it was now three o'clock. Paul decided to go back to the house and return a little later. He was expecting Tom back for the weekend and he was looking forward to seeing him again. They'd agreed to visit Diane that night too. Her condition was worsening and he knew Tom would dread the evening visit.

★ ★ ★

Tom's old banger wasn't in the drive when Paul drew up outside the house. Something must have cropped up, something important enough for him to cancel his visit to see his mother. Paul entered the kitchen and immediately he saw the note propped up against the kettle. He recognised Tom's handwriting.

The note read:

Visiting Mum. Urgent message from hospital. Tried to contact you but your mobile must have been out of range. Hope you can make it.

Love, Tom.

It was imperative he get to the hospital quickly to support Tom who would surely be finding it difficult to cope alone. Quickly turning and locking the door behind him, he jumped back into the car and pressed his foot down hard on the accelerator. The traffic was reasonably light and within minutes he drew up outside the hospital and dashed in through the front entrance.

The corridor was empty and the minute he entered the ward, stern-faced the ward sister came out of her office. That was ominous. He knew there was something wrong.

The serious look disappeared and her face softened.

'Do come in, Mr Trent. Tom is here with me. It's bad news I'm afraid.'

5

Josh and Will left college ahead of Carol. She walked across the road with Simon and he unlocked the car door ready to leave.

'Thanks for letting me in on things, Carol. The exhibition was excellent, and of course, what can I say? The news about your pictures is wonderful. I'll see you at the club next week.' He leant over and pecked her on the cheek.

As she was about to cross the road back to the college to meet up with Kim and the others she saw Paul flash past in his car. That was a pity. She was eager to know more about the mystery buyer and the commission for more pictures. But it was too late now. Paul was leaving. Maybe she should have made more attention when he told her about the sale. But he did appear to rush off.

It was a pity she hadn't been alone when Paul had told her about the buyer. They could have talked things through. But she hadn't expected him to leave so soon. And now it appeared he'd gone for the day.

Once back in the hall she spotted Kim who waved excitedly. She rushed over to Carol. 'I'm over the moon,' she said. 'It hasn't sunk in yet that I've sold a picture.'

'I know what you mean. Same here.'

'But you sold all four. That's brilliant. I must say they're lovely as a set and individually too.'

'Thanks, Kim. They were no better than yours. After all our worries about the exhibition it's turned out great in the end.' She spotted a couple more students and waved. 'What do we do now.'

'I think Paul's coming back to organise things, take away the pictures, the ones that have been sold. He said he'd see us back here.'

'I'm glad about that,' Carol said, her

spirit now brightening.

At least she'd have the chance to talk to him. 'I saw him leave as I was coming back to the hall. I assumed he'd gone for good.'

'That's not what I heard. Rita Franklin said he'd definitely be back. Come on. Let's have a coffee to celebrate.'

No sooner had they returned from the student refectory than Carol felt a tap on her shoulder. It was the secretary, Rita Franklin, herself.

'You are the Thursday group, the ones these pictures belong to, aren't you?' She looked down at a note in her hand. 'I have a message from Mr Trent. Apparently something serious has cropped up, he hasn't said what, and he's asked me to collect the 'sold' pictures and take them to the office.'

She turned to Kim. 'Do you mind taking charge? I know you've been in the group a year or two now, and you must know all the students concerned. When everyone has taken away their own pictures, I'll take the 'sold' ones ready for the buyers. If there are any pictures not collected, I need to take those too and lock them up with the rest. Is that all right?'

'That's fine, Mrs Franklin. Leave it with me. I think there's only Vince who's gone. The rest can collect theirs. It's almost four now and there aren't many people here. Shall we collect the 'sold' pictures, Carol?'

'That's a good idea. Five minutes and the place will be closing.' She turned to Mrs Franklin. 'I hope Paul's problem is nothing too serious.'

'I've no idea what is, dear,' she replied. 'All I know is that it sounded urgent.'

Carol felt a twinge of guilt. Paul had told her the buyer was a contact of his. He'd obviously steered the guy in the right direction to choose her pictures. And she hadn't even thanked him.

* * *

Tom tried to remain dispassionate about the loss of his mother. 'She died in her sleep. She wouldn't feel any pain, would she?'

'Let's hope not, Tom,' Paul said, knowing that, typical of an eighteen-year-old, Tom had built a barrier to protect himself from showing any real grief. But despite this bravado, Paul detected a confusion of emotions in Tom's eyes, knowing that, once his mother's death had registered, it wouldn't be long before the barrier collapsed.

They left the hospital and sat in silence during the car journey home. Paul garaged the car and Tom parked his in the drive.

'I'm leaving for college tomorrow morning,' Tom said. 'I've lots of revision to do. We've an end of unit test coming up next week. I don't want to fall behind.'

'But Tom, you can't go back so soon. Don't you think you should stay and help me make arrangements for your mother's funeral, show some respect and try to give her a good send-off?'

'Sorry. I know I need to be back for the funeral, but I wasn't thinking. I don't know about these things. I suppose you're right.'

That night when they talked things through, Tom broke down. Everything he'd bottled up over the years flooded out as though from a bottomless well. To him his mother was someone they visited in hospital. He'd grown up without her. His closest relative was Paul.

'I didn't have a mother like the other kids,' he sobbed. 'When I was little, I wanted to be like them, I wanted a mum.'

'I know, Tom. For all my efforts trying to make it up to you, I knew I could never replace her.'

'But I'm not criticising you. I just want you to know how I feel.'

'I realise that, Tom. It's the best way, getting it off your chest. But let's look to the positive. I know your mum wasn't there for you when you needed her, but hopefully we did manage to overcome that obstacle — as best we could. We've had some happy times together. We can't detract from that.'

Tom nodded his head and dried his eyes. Paul knew he'd feel much better once he faced up to his loss. And he'd be in a better position to cope back at university too.

They talked long into the night and it was the early hours before Tom went up to bed. But Paul needed time to pull his own thoughts together. It had been a long stretch.

Diane had been a young girl and Tom just a baby when Paul had taken on full responsibility. And whilst he'd channelled all his energies into comforting Tom after the death of his mother, Paul still needed to contend with his own grief.

Weary after an exhausting day putting the final touches to the exhibition, being there to supervise, and then discovering Diane had lost the battle, he set off upstairs. Whilst he'd known Diane had only weeks to live, losing her was so traumatic after all those years of hope.

His mind was in a whirl and his thoughts became jumbled as he reached the bedroom. He was about to get into bed when suddenly his thoughts turned to Carol. He'd not seen her to tell her about the proposal Guy had come up with.

He turned, went back downstairs and took a notepad and pen from his writing desk. After the ordeal of losing Diane, he couldn't possibly telephone Carol and discuss Guy's proposal. He would need to sound cheerful, to congratulate her. In his present state of mine that would have been impossible.

He wrote down Guy's address and telephone number suggesting Carol contact Guy as soon as possible. There was no point telling her Diane had passed away. Carol didn't know about Diane. It hadn't seem relevant to tell her. It was depressing enough for him without passing on his emotions to Carol. And the last thing he wanted was to put a damper on things when he knew she would be elated at selling the pictures.

There would be time after the funeral to phone her and talk things through. By then she would no doubt have contacted Guy.

He slipped the letter into an envelope, addressed it and placed it on the small table in the hall ready to post.

The post dropped noisily on to the doormat, most of it being the regular junk mail. Carol rifled through the envelopes and pulled out the only one that appeared to be a personal letter. Fingering it, she stared at the envelope. The writing was unfamiliar.

But there was no point standing there contemplating its source or its contents when she could so easily open it. She slipped a finger under the flap, slit the envelope and pulled out the letter from inside.

As she unfolded it a cheque fell to

the floor. She bent and picked it up. It was signed by a Guy Rollinson and its value was one hundred and sixty pounds. Her brow furrowed. Who on earth was this guy and why the cheque?

She pulled her thoughts together and unfolded the letter. A feeling of unease gripped her, causing her heart to flutter in her chest. It was from Paul.

She's been so taken up with her paintings and the fact that all four had sold so quickly that she'd neglected him on the Saturday. She should have followed him out and talked things through with him before he dashed off.

The letter read:

Dear Carol

Sorry I didn't see you again after our brief meeting on Saturday. I intended returning to the exhibition, but unfortunately something urgent cropped up and I couldn't get back there. A friend of mine, Guy Rollinson, a gallery owner, bought your pictures. He'd like more. I enclose his cheque.

Perhaps if I give you his address and telephone number you could contact him direct at his Westerton Gallery. The phone number is Westerton 379642.

It's unlikely I'll be with you on Thursday, and after that I believe Katie will be back to take over the class. I wish you every success for the future, especially in your dealings with Guy. I am extremely proud of you. Success will certainly come your way if you start to believe in yourself.

Kind regards
Paul

Carol's stomach gave a nosedive. Unless she contacted Paul, it looked as though she wouldn't see him again. She felt so ungrateful. Was this the way to end their relationship after all the encouragement he'd given her?

She must telephone and ask to meet up with him. But perhaps she should contact Guy Rollinson first to give her a valid reason to telephone Paul.

She went into the lounge and dialled the number. It was Guy himself who answered. When she broached the subject of the exhibition and her pictures he suggested they meet rather than discuss business over the telephone.

It turned out that Guy owned three places in North Yorkshire, two of which were galleries, one in Harrogate, the other in Westerton, and a souvenir shop in Bishopdale.

'I'd like you to paint two more sets of four florals, eight in all, making a total of twelve including the ones I've already bought. I plan to take prints of them all and sell them in the Westerton gallery and the Bishopdale shop. The originals I'd like to keep for the Harrogate gallery. What do you think?' he asked her.

'I just can't believe you're so interested,' she said wide-eyed with astonishment.

'They'll go down well in the galleries,

Carol, and I'm prepared to give you a fair price for them. We'll see what interest we get in Harrogate and if the originals go quickly, which I'm convinced they will, I'll commission more.'

'That's wonderful, Guy. I'm really grateful you've chosen my work.'

'This is business purely and simply my dear. All I need now is the pictures. I'm anxious to get them framed and put on display.'

Carol almost skipped as she left the gallery later on. And then the thought struck her that, to give the commission a fair shot, she would need plenty of time to develop the compositions. The pictures had to be spot-on. But she couldn't afford to do fewer hours for Barron & Weeks, the pictures weren't sure to sell.

Something would have to give. She'd need to give *Images* a miss for a week or so until she'd completed the paintings.

She parked the car in the garage and went inside the house. Fired with excitement, she picked up the telephone and dialled Paul's number. The phone rang for some time before it was answered. The voice at the other end was a woman's. Carol asked to speak to Paul.

'I'm sorry Paul is at Diane's funeral this afternoon. Can I take a message?'

Carol was taken aback. She knew nothing about Diane or a funeral.

'I do apologise. I didn't realise. I'll telephone next week. There's no need to pass on a message.'

'That might be for the best, dear,' the woman offered. 'You can imagine how upset they are, especially Tom at losing his mother. Paul will have a lot on his plate. But if you'd like me to scribble a note for him . . . '

'That's very kind of you, but it's not important. Thank you all the same.'

Carol gently replaced the receiver. She could barely believe it. Paul had had a wife all along. Her head reeled and her stomach churned violently. Why had he invited her out without telling her of his circumstances?

Her mind was filled with questions. A multitude of emotions flowed. Sorrow that Paul had lost his wife. But jealousy that he'd had a wife at all, especially when her own feelings for him had been a driving force she'd found difficult to deny, something she could only now admit to herself.

But who was she to judge when she didn't know the circumstances. And worst of all, she was thinking about herself once more.

Her only option was to write to Paul. He must be feeling dreadful. And what of Tom, how must he be feeling? There she was jaunting off to Harrogate, discussing business with Guy whilst Paul and Tom were grieving.

She picked up a pen and notepad and started to write. But she stopped suddenly. How could she mention his wife, Diane when he'd never disclosed he had a wife? She would have to offer her condolences without reference to anyone in particular. She wrote:

Dear Paul

Thank you for your letter and the cheque from Guy Rollinson. I was sorry not to have seen you when we went back to the exhibition after lunch, but we were told by Mrs Franklin that something urgent had cropped up. I telephoned your house today to tell you about my meeting with Guy, and I was sorry to hear you were attending a funeral.

I hope we can meet up some time, at your convenience of course. I'd like to explain the outcome of my meeting with Guy. I can't thank you enough for all the help you've given me. We shall all miss you at the class.

Kind regards
Carol

She felt a desperate need to see Paul and offer some comfort, even though it was his wife who had died. But who was the woman on the phone? By the sound of her voice she was someone older.

Carol read the letter through again. It

was only brief, but what more could she say? All she could hope now was that Paul would contact her at some future date when she could tell him of the progress with Guy Rollinson.

* * *

Paul steeled himself to be strong on the grey day Diane was laid to rest in the little churchyard in Westerton. Tom had tried hard too, but he needed Paul's support to remain stable throughout the service. Afterwards just a few people had returned to the house where his good friend and neighbour, Marion Brunswick, had kindly prepared a meal. He owed her so much. She'd been a treasure to him, supporting and helping him since Tom's childhood days.

'It's over, Tom,' Paul had murmured when the last of the mourners had left. 'We need a fresh start. Even though we're grieving, your mum wouldn't want us to be miserable. You see, she was so lively when she was younger. I'm sorry you never really knew her, Tom. But you do take after her. You're so vibrant and focused. She was really bright when she was a young girl. And talented too,'

'You've never told me that before, not in so many words.'

'It's true, Tom. Diane still lives, in you. And that makes me truly happy.'

Tom's reluctance to face his mother's plight had led to feelings of guilt, but now she was gone he was starting to come to terms with it and, after the funeral and his lengthy conversations with Paul, much of that guilt had been dispersed.

After Tom's return to university, Paul felt desperately lonely. There was still George's portrait to start, but the motivation wasn't there.

And then it struck him that, through all his own grieving and his concern for Tom too, whilst he'd not forgotten Carol, he'd done nothing about the letter she'd sent him. He'd not even acknowledged it let alone telephoned her to make arrangements to meet. But he knew she'd understand. She was that sort of woman.

He picked up the letter and dialled her number. But there was no reply. He tried to hazard a guess as to where she might be. She certainly wasn't working at her desk that day which he knew to be her usual routine, otherwise she'd have picked up the phone immediately. Maybe she was at the club. Maybe she was there with that man.

The thought triggered a twinge of jealousy and he tried to cast the man's image from his mind. Why should he be jealous? He had no claim on Carol, and he hadn't intimated he'd like a commitment. So why shouldn't she be there with that man?

After his initial disappointment that Carol had not replied when he'd phoned, he felt he needed to get out of the house, do something different. He went into the hall and took his woollen overcoat from the cloakroom.

The telephone started to ring as he

made to open the front door. Should he bother to go back and answer it? He couldn't face up to anyone else asking how he was, or offering their condolences. They were kind gestures. but there was only so much he could take.

He closed the door and strode across the hall. His decision made, he lifted the receiver.

'Paul Trent.'

'Hello Paul. It's Carol here.'

* * *

Two pictures complete, Carol started on a third. Just as she was finishing off the background wash, the telephone began to ring. But at that precise moment she couldn't answer it otherwise the wash would be ruined. She could hear someone leaving a message on the answer phone. It could be someone important ringing her.

She left the wash to dry and ran back the tape. It was Paul. Should she ring back? It was going to be difficult because she knew there'd been the funeral the woman on the phone had mentioned. Maybe it would be better if she didn't refer to it. Maybe she should let Paul tell her what had happened. She picked up the telephone and dialled the number.

'Lovely to hear from you, Carol,' Paul replied.

'Sorry I couldn't answer the phone. I was in the middle of a background wash.'

'I understand. I was about to leave the house. But I'm sure we've lots to talk about. What are you doing right now?'

'Painting, Paul. That's all I seem to do these days.'

'Do I sense it's becoming a bore, having to press on with the painting?'

'Not at all, I love it. But sometimes I need to push myself to take a break. I haven't been to *Images* for a couple of weeks.

'Oh dear. Don't tell me you're not keeping up the fitness.'

Carol laughed. 'I'm afraid not. I don't have the time.'

'How about a brisk walk over the moor? I'm sure we've lots to talk about, and it should make up for some of the lack of exercise,' he said. 'Surely you can break off for a couple of hours. I could be over there in twenty minutes. What do you think?'

'Sounds great. Just what I need. See you in twenty minutes.'

Although she felt Paul had deceived her, she still wanted him — and too much for comfort. But that was wrong. They should never have been out together when Paul had a wife at home. Carol wasn't that sort of woman. But her heart began to flutter at the thought of seeing him again.

She cleaned her paint brushes, put them away and took a pair of warm trousers and her calf length boots from the wardrobe. There was a chill in the air and she needed to protect herself from the sneaky winds blowing across the moor. By the time she'd wound a scarf around her neck and slipped on her coat, the doorbell rang.

It was Paul, his broad smile in no way disguising the tiredness around his eyes. A blast of sorrow pierced her heart. She wanted to reach out and pull him towards her. He looked like a little boy, and he needed comfort.

'Nice seeing you again, Paul. Sorry I missed you at the exhibition.' She said, trying to control the emotion seeping from within.

Paul stretched across and gave her a peck on the cheek. 'Good to see you too. Let's take the car to the edge of the moor and leave it there. We've a lot to catch up on.' He took hold of her hand and led her to the car.

They set off up the road and sat in comfortable silence until they reached the moor. Paul parked the car and turned to her, his face a mask of sorrow.

'Before you fill me in about Guy and the paintings, there's something I need to tell you.' He swallowed hard and his eyes welled with tears. 'We lost my sister, Diane, a couple of weeks ago. Tom's had a terrible time coming to terms with it. But we're winning, he's back at university now.'

Carol gasped. 'Your sister? I'm dreadfully sorry, Paul. I didn't know you had a sister. The woman who answered just told me you were at a funeral.'

'Marion Brunswick, a very kind lady. We couldn't have coped without her.' He paused. 'I realise now I've not told you about my sister. It was on the tip of my tongue when we met at Bellini's, but you told me about Mike and I didn't want to follow by telling you about Diane. And, of course, I thought Josh may have mentioned it.'

'Josh didn't know I'm sure of that. He still thinks Tom's your son.'

'There you go. It's obvious you can't make assumptions.'

She opened her mouth to speak, but Paul continued.

'Hear me out, Carol. At least for you

it was over when you lost Mike. But not for us.' He paused. 'You've realised now that Tom's not my son. He's my nephew, my sister, Diane's, boy. Diane married Tom's father, Rob when they were both eighteen. They were at college together, studying art.' He smiled. 'It runs in the family you see,' he added lightly.

'Within the year Tom was born but Diane suffered from post-natal depression. She was taken to hospital for treatment, but her condition worsened. She developed a more serious illness from which she never recovered. We brought her home several times but we just couldn't cope. She was permanently in care where she had the best of treatment.'

'At first she knew who we were, but then she didn't recognise either Tom or me. It was very sad. Her condition gradually deteriorated. And then she developed Alzheimer's and the consultant gave her only months to live,' he said, his voice wavering. 'She was so young, not yet forty. The consultant told us it was unusual. But what help was that to us?' He shook his head and shrugged his shoulders.

'Tom buried his head in the sand. He didn't want to know. But that's typical of a boy his age. Of course he made an effort, but I knew he was reluctant. He never really knew his mother. To him I'm his only relative, the one he grew up with.'

Carol took his hand. 'Oh, Paul, that's terrible. But what about Tom's father?'

'Rob severed all links shortly after Diane was diagnosed. He couldn't cope. He disappeared from college and he hasn't been seen since. At the time he was only nineteen. Tom was six weeks old the last time Rob set eyes on him.'

'I would never have known he wasn't your son. You have a very close relationship. But I'm so sorry about your sister. It must have been such an ordeal visiting the hospital and not knowing how things would be when you arrived.'

'It was. And what made it worse was that I didn't have Tom to go along with me towards the end, except when he was back from university. When we visited together we always tried to have a conversation in the hope that Diane would take in some of what we were saying. But going alone it wasn't easy.'

'I understand that.'

'At least Tom seems to be coming to terms with it now that he's more mature. When he was fifteen, he became moody and then the trouble started at school. That problem took some handling believe you me, but he seems to be over it now, on the surface at least. You see, since he was a little boy, he's been desperate to be like his friends and have a mother who was there for him.'

'Paul, that's so sad. I know what you mean. At least Josh and I could grieve. We know Mike's gone for ever. It's final. But for you . . . '

'Let's not go there,' Paul said, and Carol felt he was restraining himself from showing any more emotion.

'I don't know anyone who could have coped the way you have, Paul.'

'It has been difficult. I just haven't had the time for anything serious. Don't get me wrong. Since Tom was old enough not to need my constant attention, I have had relationships, but I've not wanted to impose anyone on him. He's always come first. And once I became so used to being on my own, I must admit I enjoyed my independence.'

'I couldn't agree more,' she said. 'Making decisions without having to consult anyone. And Josh is so easy to please. Although, having said that, it won't last much longer. He seems to be asserting himself more and more since he started on his college course.'

'But now that I've off-loaded let's get on to something lighter. How have things gone for you? With Guy I mean.'

'Unbelievably well. And I'm really grateful to you for all your encouragement.'

'It's nothing to do with me. You were spotted as having potential. Guy's no fool.'

'He asked me to produce two more sets of florals, eight all together. I've already started the first set,' she said and gave him a detailed account of her discussion with Guy. 'So I'll need to hold my breath and see what happens.'

'I'm delighted for you,' Paul repeated and he slipped his arm around her waist and squeezed her. 'Well done,' he added, but to Carol's disappointment he quickly removed his arm. She realised she was reading too much into his words and gestures. Maybe he was congratulating her as he would a pupil he'd taught.

'There's one thing I won't do,' he continued. 'I've no intention of viewing your work until it's complete and on display in the gallery. You're on your own now. Decide on your compositions and stick to them. And if you take my advice you won't show them to anyone else. You don't need other people's ideas or criticisms. They're your master-pieces. It's your decision that counts.'

'That sounds like good advice,' Carol replied as she wrapped her slim arms round her body against the whiplash of the cold wind. 'But they're hardly masterpieces.'

Paul ignored her last comment and slipped his arm around her shoulder, rubbing the top of her arm.

'Maybe we should turn back now. You're looking cold.'

Her stomach did a somersault. But she knew she shouldn't be feeling like this. She must try to control herself. He needed to grieve, and he'd said his independence was important to him, which meant he definitely wasn't available and that was that.

6

Carol desperately needed every minute she could find to complete the pictures for Guy. She'd worked on them all day and had a break for the evening meal, but Josh had gone out with Will and she decided to continue until he came back.

It was after seven when she went upstairs into the spare room she'd been using as her studio. Anxious to get on, she picked up her pencil to sketch the flowers on the final picture of the first set. At that moment, the door bell rang and a ripple of annoyance caused her to frown.

Popping her pencil to one side, she went downstairs into the hall and opened the front door. Her stomach sank. Simon was standing there on the doorstep. But realising it was selfish of her to feel resentful she hastily put on a smile.

'Simon, nice to see you,' she said, hoping her disappointment wasn't apparent.

'I'm glad I've caught you in, Carol,' he said. 'I've been wondering what had happened to you.'

Carol backed off in surprise. 'I'm still here,' she said laughing. 'But painting is my priority at the moment. That's why I haven't been to the club recently,' she said.

'Painting? I see,' he said, his forehead creasing in a look of puzzlement. And then he stepped forward. 'Do I have to stand here in the freezing cold on the doorstep or are you going to ask me in?' he added, a smile now replacing the frown.

He was certainly being up-front. But perhaps she was being tetchy at having been disturbed.

'Sorry, you took me by surprise, Simon. Do come in,' she said, groaning inside, and knowing she would have to work extra hard that evening to complete the final picture of the set. 'Would you like a coffee or perhaps a cup of tea?' she asked him, secretly hoping he'd refuse. She was itching to get on with the sketches.

'I'd love a coffee,' he replied, following her through to the kitchen. 'Now what's all this about spending your time painting?'

'Remember the pictures I sold at the exhibition?' she said, her eyes aglow with excitement.

'I do indeed. That was good news. I told you so at the time.'

'I've been asked to do more,' she told him. 'It's such a challenge.'

'I suppose it is, but surely not at the expense of everything else. What about the club? At our age, we need to keep that up,' he offered, an obsequious smile sketching his face. 'And it's all of three weeks since I've seen you,' he complained.

Carol laughed, not sure whether or not he was being serious. 'I can't do both, Simon. I'm on trial so to speak,' she said spooning coffee into the cafetiere and pouring on boiling water.

'If these first pictures sell, then he'll probably want more.'

'He'll want more?' Simon repeated. 'Who's he?'

'Guy Rollinson. He has two quite prestigious galleries and a souvenir shop. He seems to be very interested.'

'Good for you,' he said, his reply patronising. 'Now, when are we going to have that night out?' he asked, quickly changing the subject. 'Don't tell me you're too busy to spare me a night,' he said. Carol detected a note of cynicism in his voice.

'Honestly, Simon. I've so much to do I can't possibly break off just yet for a night out. Maybe in a couple of weeks' time.'

'A couple of week's time! It surprises me you're making a big issue of this picture lark. You'll probably get peanuts for them anyway. Don't you think you'd be better off sticking to your day job? Your pictures are all very nice, love, but they're hardly going to make you a fortune.'

Carol saw red. Supercilious, chauvinistic, egocentric prig! Her choice of adjectives was endless. She could have gone on. Who on earth did he think he was, giving his opinion? A condescending one too. He wasn't talking to a simpleton of a woman.

'I beg your pardon, Simon, but I'll be the judge of whether I wish to sell my pictures or not. And for your information I've already signed an agreement with Guy. You might not think the commission lucrative, but I happen to think it is.'

'Don't take it the wrong way, love. What I'm saying is for your own sake. I know what you women are like. You get a bee in your bonnet about something and then you go overboard.' He laughed his false little laugh once more.

Carol was becoming more and more agitated but she tried desperately to control any visible emotion. First of all he was being over-familiar and secondly he knew very little about her, certainly not enough to be giving his opinion as to what was and what was not right for her.

It wasn't surprising his wife had gone off on tour. He'd probably criticised her singing.

'I'm not one of the typical women you're referring to. What on earth has come over you? I thought we were good friends. I believed I had a supporter in you.'

'We are good friends, Carol, but surely I'm entitled to offer you advice. Surely that's what friends are for.'

She steeled herself and held back the words she really wanted to say.

'I'm afraid that's not the sort of advice I need,' she said. 'I'm committed to completing the work and I must devote as much time as possible to doing so.'

She drained her cup and stood up. Simon followed suit and placed his cup on the table. 'Sorry if we got at loggerheads, love. I didn't mean to upset you,' he said turning and going through into the hall. He slipped his car keys from his jacket pocket. 'You won't forget the invite will you? I didn't take you for one of these modern women who don't like to be wined and dined by us guys,' he said, a challenging look in his eyes.

'Why do you need to earn extra money, Carol, when that's what we men are here for?' He laughed and reached out to open the door, but Carol stepped ahead and opened it for him.

'It's not necessarily the money, it's the challenge. And I'm not in the habit of sponging off anyone, Simon,' she stressed, the flush of irritation rising to her cheeks. 'Money aside, I hope you understand I'm serious about the pictures.'

He turned to her, took her hand. 'Of course you are,' he replied, a caustic edge to his tone. He slid his hands to her wrists and pulled her roughly towards him, pressing his lips to hers.

And then he smiled and left the house.

Carol stood there astounded by the

arrogance of the man. If he thought she was going to spend an evening listening to his Victorian ideas on the woman's place and the woman's intellect, then he could think again. What would Paul think if he heard the guy criticising her for being enthusiastic about her painting?

As Paul neared the house a kind of excitement engulfed him. Perhaps he should have telephoned first. But he didn't expect to stay. He realised how much time she needed to complete the picture Guy had commissioned. All he wanted was to ask her out as soon as she had an evening to spare.

He drew up outside and opened the car ready to step out. And then he saw it. The silver BMW sports car parked in the drive. It was the one belonging to that guy.

Paul told himself he'd chosen the wrong evening to call. He stepped smartly back into his car, gently closed the door and turned on the ignition. He was about to drive away when the front door to Carol's house opened, spilling light on to the drive. Hoping not to be seen, Paul slid down in his seat.

There were silhouetted in the doorway, Carol and the guy. He was kissing her. Paul was gripped by tension. That was it, his cue to leave. The last thing he wanted to cramp their style.

Disappointed, he felt on edge as he drove back home. Fair enough he had wanted to have a word with Carol, but he'd desperately wanted to see her again too. He'd kept on trying to convince himself it was only a friendship, despite having felt so cosy with her the last time they'd been together. But things weren't always what they appeared.

He knew he would never get over losing Diane. He missed her dearly. But she wouldn't have wanted him to be miserable and since his stroll on the moors with Carol a few days earlier, he'd bucked himself up. He'd made arrangements for George to come for a sitting and he'd been satisfied at the results.

The telephone was ringing as he opened the door. It was his agent, Rick.

'Another commission from Steinbeck's, Paul. I need to discuss it with you. It's something different this time. I've had a few ideas floating around in my head. I wondered if you'd be free tomorrow.'

'Tomorrow's fine, Rick, but not until the afternoon. George Peel will be here for another sitting in the morning. I'll come over about two if that suits.'

'That's settled then. By the way, the student you recommended, Carol Henderson, I saw her work in Guy Rollinson's gallery in Harrogate. We could have a bright new spark there. Do you have phone number? I'll give her a ring.'

'I do, Rick, but I know she's in the middle of producing pictures for Guy just now. I don't know how seriously she's taking things. But it's worth a try.'

'We'll talk it through tomorrow. I'll see you then.'

Paul sat down and smiled to himself. Good old Carol. She was certainly impressing them with her work. He could only hope she wasn't becoming too involved in her private life at the expense of her future.

★ ★ ★

Carol was stinging from her reaction to Simon's attitude. Now she had the measure of him. If he thought he could step in and make arrangements for another night out he could think again. He was the type of guy she could well live without. After all she'd brought up Josh single-handedly.

As she turned to go back into the kitchen, she caught her shoe on something. A small black wallet skidded along the carpet. She bent down to pick it up. It was a credit card wallet with five cards inside, all of them in different names, but none in Simon's. That was strange.

The wallet must have been caught up in the keys when he pulled them out of his pocket. Unless of course he'd dropped them deliberately in the hope she'd chase him up at the club to give them back to him. But why would he be carrying credit cards belonging to someone else?

The answer came to her quickly. They obviously belong to his staff members, the ones who needed credit cards to cover business expenses. But why did Simon have them?

There was one thing for certain, he could forget his little game. She had no intention of meeting up with him at the club to give them back and she had no idea where he lived. In any case, she'd made a decision. She wasn't prepared to become involved in anything personal. Not any more. Her mind was made up.

She decided to look up the company telephone number and speak to the receptionist there. It was probably a coward's way out, but she didn't care. Simon was the last person she wanted to see after the way he'd behaved.

He'd said his company was in

Sheffield, but when she rang directory enquiries, they had no reference to the company *Fast Gear*, in Sheffield. Maybe it was in the Chesterfield directory or one of the towns within that radius. But Carol had no joy.

She decided to look on the web and see if there was an address there. Finally she came up with a company in Nottingham. It puzzled her. The way he'd talked about *Fast Gear* it wasn't too far away, south of Sheffield had been his words. It seemed quite strange that he should be based in Leeds which must be eighty miles away from Nottingham. Surely he didn't travel there and back every day.

But at least she had the telephone number as a last resort.

By the end of the week, she'd completed the first set of pictures and started on the second. Guy Rollinson was delighted.

'These are wonderful, Carol,' he said standing the pictures up against the wall and viewing them from a distance.

'They're even better than I'd imagined.'

'I'm glad you like them. I'm relieved too, but I'd better not hang around. I've made a start with the second set and I need to get on.'

'Give me a ring when you've finished them. I'll come over and collect them, save you the time travelling here. I appreciate you're getting behind with other things,' he said.

'That's right, Guy. I can't afford to give up my work with Barron and Weeks until I'm sure things are going well with the paintings. And even then I'll only cut down on the hours. I can't give up altogether. I need something to fall back on.'

'I'm sure that's a sensible way to look at it, Carol. But before you go I'll give you a cheque for this set and the balance when you complete.'

'I must say that's prompt and it's very much appreciated,' she said fingering the cheque and thinking what an idiot Simon had been expecting her to give up her painting just to give him the pleasure of seeing her at the club.

She was flattering herself of course, intimating he found it a pleasure, but he was coming on strong and that wasn't part of their agreement. He had said no strings and that's what she'd expected. But the kiss put an end to it as far as she was concerned. How dare he take such a liberty?

At the door, Guy concluded, 'I'm looking forward to the next batch. If they're as good as these, we're home and dry. I'm sure I'll have no problems selling them.'

On the way home her earlier thoughts about Simon and his foolish comments brought into focus the credit cards. Still she'd done nothing with them and yet her earlier decision stood. She didn't want to see Simon at the club. He'd surely get the wrong impression. Perhaps she could call in there, explain to reception she needed to freeze her membership temporarily and ask if them if they would hand over the cards to Simon when next they saw him. That would solve her problem.

'We're not supposed to play messenger,' the receptionist told her. 'There could be something lethal in the envelope for all I know.'

Carol tore it open. 'Here, look. They're credit cards. He dropped them when he called to see me. He may need them.'

'Seeing you've explained, I'll do it for you on this occasion.' She slipped her hand underneath the counter. 'Here's another envelope. Put them in, seal it up. I'd offer to give you his address, but I'd really be in trouble if they found out.'

Carol sealed the envelope and passed it over. 'I realise that, Janine. Thanks for doing it. You know where I am if you need me,' she said.

Josh had returned from college when she arrived home. She opened the door and waved the cheque in the air, taking his hands and doing a little jig.

'Mum, you're being silly again,' he wailed, freeing himself from her grip.

'What's that you're waving in the air? If anyone walked in they'd think you were off your trolley.'

'I might be at that, too,' she said, laughing. 'What's this, you ask?' she continued, placing the cheque on the table and smoothing her hand over it. 'It's the income from my work as an artist of course.'

Josh picked up the cheque and stared. 'Mum this is brill. I can't believe it. I'll take back what I said. You're still Top Mum,' he said giving her a squeeze.

'Well it's no good to me hovering about here, I've work to do. But how about if we go into the city this evening and have a meal at the Indian?' There was so much to do she knew she shouldn't, but she felt she needed quality time with Josh.

'Good thinking, Mum. I'll do my course work whilst you're painting and then I'll get ready. About seven, do you think?'

The telephone rang later as Carol

picked up her brush to continue with the painting.

It was Rick Golding, Paul's agent. Carol was amazed that he'd asked to meet her with a view to discussing her future.

'I appreciate the call, Rick, but could you give me a couple of days to finish the commission for Guy Rollinson?'

'There's no hurry,' he said. 'Paul told me you were up to your eyes in work. Give me a ring when the pictures are finished.'

The conversation triggered thoughts of Paul. She enjoyed their time together and he'd promised to telephone her. That was a couple of weeks ago. Perhaps he too was busy. But now she wanted to thank Paul for recommending her to Rick. And although she didn't want to appear pushy, she decided to invite him over for a meal.

She picked up the phone and dialled his number. Butterflies flittered in her stomach and her heart started to race. She was being silly again.

'Paul Trent,' he said, and for a few seconds Carol seemed lost for words. And then she pulled herself together.

'It's me, Carol,' she replied tentatively. 'I wondered if you'd be free to come for dinner one evening next week. I'm hoping to have completed the pictures by then and I've had a call from Rick Golding.'

'That would be nice, but I'm pretty tied up most of the week.'

'How about Saturday?'

'That would be perfect. What time?'

'About seven? Can you manage that?' she asked.

'I sure can. I'm looking forward to seeing you, Carol. And hearing about your work.'

She replaced the receiver. Everything was happening at once. First she receives a handsome payment for the pictures, then an agent calls wanting to represent her, and best of all Paul agrees to have dinner with her.

No sooner had Carol put the phone back on the hook than it rang again. It was the receptionist at *Images*.

'Mrs Henderson?'

'Carol Henderson speaking.'

'Carol, it's Janine, *Images*. I phoned Simon Rothwell about the envelope. His phone was dead. It seems he's moved away, or he's not paid the bill. But that's hardly likely. He seemed to be quite well off. Could you call in and collect the envelope? There's not much point leaving it here. Sorry I couldn't pass it on.'

'Thanks for trying, Janine. He didn't say anything about moving the last time I saw him. That's strange.'

Carol felt her stomach lurch. Now she was stuck with the credit cards. Where on earth had Simon disappeared to?

'That was wicked, Mum,' Josh said as they left the Indian later that night. 'You ought to get a cheque more regularly and then we could eat like that every day.'

'You mean you're not happy with my cooking?' she said, covering her mouth to stifle her giggles.

'You know what I mean, Mum.'

It was quite late when they arrived home, too late for Carol to start painting. 'I'm going to watch T.V. for half an hour, love. Then I think I'll have an early night.'

'That's fine by me. I must finish my maths homework.'

Carol switched on the TV and relaxed in an armchair. The news had started, but she fancied something lighter, something more entertaining. She picked up the control and was about to switch to a different channel when her attention was drawn to a news item, about credit card cloning. As a police officer started to explain the technique, she became intrigued.

'The fraudsters enlist shop assistants and petrol station clerks who copy details of credit cards by using a magnetic card stripe reader, a sophisticated gadget usually clipped to a belt.'

The officer held up a sample of the small gadget.

147

'All that is needed is a furtive swipe of the card, obviously out of view of the customer. The cards are later cloned using the details from the magnetic stripes.'

The newsreader continued with the story, reporting that credit card companies were losing millions of pounds a year and as a result, in addition to the police investigations, the companies themselves had employed their own anti-fraud teams.

The item triggered off thoughts of the cards now in Carol's possession, those left behind by Simon. If he'd heard this particular news item about the cloning, he'd be worried once he realised his company cards were missing in case they landed in the wrong hands. He'd surely be anxious to get them back.

Perhaps she should try the *Fast Gear* phone number in Nottingham. She could speak to the receptionist without getting involved with Simon himself. Alternatively she could post them on.

But maybe that wasn't a good idea after all. They could be intercepted in the post. Whatever happened she must get them back to him pretty quickly and avoid the possibility of any more contact.

The next morning, although she didn't relish the thought of ringing the company, having tried to avoid this scenario, now that she'd made up her mind, she decided to ring immediately and get it over with. She picked up the phone, dialled the number and started to explain about the credit cards to the receptionist.

'I think it might be better if you had a word with Mr Rothwell himself. He's in the office this morning. Hold the line.'

Without giving Carol the chance to make up an excuse not to speak to Simon, the receptionist left her on hold.

'Rothwell here.' The voice at the other end of the line was brusque. Carol barely recognised it as Simon's.

'Simon, it's Carol. You dropped a credit card wallet in my house,' she told him. 'I left it at the club, but they couldn't get in touch with you. Would you like me to post it to you or could someone collect it?'

'Sorry, my dear,' came the reply. 'I've no idea who you are or what you're talking about.'

'Are you saying you're not Simon Rothwell, a member of *Images* in Leeds?'

'We seem to be getting at cross purposes. I am Simon Rothwell, but I know nothing about *Images*, whatever that might be.'

'It's a health club. But I do apologise, Mr Rothwell. I've obviously got the wrong number and the wrong person, although the Simon Rothwell I know did say he owned a company called *Fast Gear*.'

Carol put the phone back on the hook. This was becoming a mystery. First of all she discovers Simon's telephone is cut off and then she telephones *Fast Gear* only to find that it's the wrong Simon Rothwell.

There was something very much amiss. She looked down at the credit cards, fingering them and wondering what to do next. Surely Simon would have collected them had they been important to him.

It was a pity she couldn't have found out more about him from *Images*. His address would have been useful. She could at least have posted the cards through the letter box. But it was no use speculating. Those were the rules. They didn't give out personal details.

Her only option now was to go to the police and hand the cards in. There was no way she wanted any further responsibility for them. If Simon did happen to call on her at some future date she would tell him straight that she'd been worried about the cards and her only option had been to ask the police to check up with the card companies and return them to their rightful owners.

7

Once the commission was complete, Guy came across to collect the pictures. 'Spot-on, Carol,' he said. 'We can't fail, I'm sure.'

The second cheque gave her that little bit more flexibility, and Carol decided she could afford to buy steaks for the meal she was preparing for Paul.

At last it was Saturday and, on tenterhooks hoping that nothing would go wrong, she sighed with relief as she slipped off her apron. The sound of the doorbell startled her. Her heart gave a little skip.

He was there on the doorstep looking more handsome than ever, the light dancing in his eyes as he leant forward to hug her and give her a peck on the cheek.

'It's lovely to see you again, Carol. You've been busy I take it. And you're probably going to tell me it's all my fault.' He grinned impishly.

She felt a hot flush spread to her cheeks. 'You're wrong there, Paul. I couldn't be more grateful,' she told him and her huge brown eyes focused on his.

He edged a little closer. 'You're looking radiant,' he said taking in the little black dress which fitted snugly to her body and outlined her slim figure.

'It's kind of you to say so, Paul,' she replied, now trying to control the wavering in her voice, her feelings a driving force she found difficult to deny.

'I don't know what the prescription is, but I wouldn't mind a dollop of it myself,' he added looking a little doleful.

'Oh, Paul it was remiss of me not to ask you. Are you feeling any better? And how's Tom? Is he coming to terms with losing his Mum?'

'One minute we're fine and the next — well I'm sure you know what I mean.'

'I do. That's the way I felt after I lost Mike. But I had Josh to take care of, and I had to be strong for both of us,' she said. 'You'll pull round eventually, but it takes time,' she added. She smiled. 'But let's not dwell on it. Let's get down to this evening's priorities. How do you like your steak?'

'Steak? What a treat. Medium rare for me. We're getting prosperous now.'

'A little better off admittedly,' Carol told him. 'This is a celebration to thank you for everything you've done for me.'

'I haven't done anything yet,' he said, blatantly making eyes at her.

'You're a fool, Paul,' she said and giggled.

Paul took her hand and pulled her towards him. 'I mean it, Carol'. His words were firm and brisk. 'I think you know how I feel about you.'

She felt safe in his arms, and she couldn't find the energy to draw herself away. The scent of his aftershave, that faint hint of musk made her pulses race faster. But she was being silly again.

Hadn't he once hinted he valued his independence? No matter how he felt, a relationship without commitment wasn't for her.

And it was becoming too serious. There was nothing she would like more than to snuggle up in his arms, but she knew there was so much danger in that. She couldn't afford to lose her heart to anyone, especially for purely physical reasons. Her relationship with Mike had been so wonderful that it would be difficult for anyone to take his place.

'Now,' she said, easing herself away, ignoring his comment and changing the subject. 'I need to serve the starter. It's a fish platter. I hope you like it,' she said.

'Like it? I'll enjoy anything you serve,' he replied, grinning boyishly. 'It's so good for someone else to cook for me.'

At that moment the door opened and Josh rushed into the room.

'Hello, Paul,' he said and smiled. Then he turned to Carol. 'Hope I'm not disturbing anything,' he added sheepishly, 'but I forgot my wallet.' He ran upstairs and came back down with the wallet in his hand. 'Must dash. Will's waiting for me at the bus stop.'

As he disappeared Carol and Paul started to laugh. 'There you go, Carol.' Paul took her hand again. 'I wonder what he was expecting to disturb,' he said, rolling his eyes in a dramatic gesture.

'We'll never start our meal at this rate,' Carol said, patting him on the cheek. 'Come along, into the dining room,' she ordered in pedantic tone, still holding his hand and pulling him after her.

'By the way, you said Rick Golding contacted you.'

'He did. I told him I'd get back to him as soon as Guy's pictures were finished. I was thinking of getting in touch after the weekend.'

'Good idea, Carol. He knows what the public want. You could go a long way if you stick with him.'

'I can't believe this is happening to me,' she told Paul. 'It's what, about five months since I started at the art class? Things have happened so quickly.'

'One break. That's all you needed to get off the mark.'

They had so much to talk about that by the time they moved away from the table, Josh had returned.

'You're still here, Paul,' Josh said, giving him a knowing look.

'We got carried away with one thing and another. I didn't realise the time.'

'Don't rush off on my account,' Josh said. 'How's Tom, by the way. I must contact him when he's back again. I was sorry to hear about his mum.'

'Yes it was very sad, but he's taking things in his stride, Josh. In the circumstances, he's doing well.'

Josh turned to Carol. 'I'm going to bed, Mum. I need to be up early in the morning. Will and I are going out for the day.' He blushed.

'I see,' Carol said, knowing there was

something afoot. 'Just you and Will?'

'A few of us,' he said, and he turned to go upstairs. 'See you around, Paul.'

Carol smiled to herself. Josh was keeping something a secret. Maybe it was a girl!

'You must come to my place next time, Carol,' Paul insisted as he stood there ready to leave, his slow devastating grin reaching his eyes. And then he leant forward and kissed her gently, drawing her into a dreamy sensation that clouded her mind and wormed her body to a radiant glow.

'I'd like that,' she said, her mind spinning from the kiss.

Carol felt highly satisfied that she'd done herself proud. The meal had gone wonderfully well and she knew Paul had enjoyed it.

He opened the door and stepped out into the night. As he reversed his car out of the drive he waved from his window, his headlights picking up the shape of a waiting car a few yards down the road. It was a police car.

* ★ ★ ★

'The sergeant told me you'd called in. How long had you known Rothwell, Mrs Henderson?'

'Just a few weeks,' she said. 'We met at the health club, *Images*. But why are you asking me that?'

'We'd like you to help us with our enquiries. You say he dropped the credit cards whilst he was here at your house. What was the purpose of his visit?'

'He wanted to know why I hadn't been to the club, nothing more.'

'But he hasn't been there himself for over a week.'

'So I gather. But it's no business of mine whether he's been there or not.'

'I'm afraid we'll have to ask you to come down to the station, Mrs Henderson. This business is far more complex than it appears. From our enquiries you were seen out with him at *La Rue* in Boroughton, just a few weeks ago.'

'But it was a one-off. It's the only

time I've ever been out with him.'

'Even so, there are one or two things we need to iron out,' the constable told her.

'But I can't leave my son here alone.'

'Your son? How old is he and where is he?'

'He's sixteen and he's in bed.'

'With all due respect Mrs Henderson, at sixteen he's old enough to stay on his own for an hour or two.'

Carol couldn't believe what was happening but, not wanting to alarm Josh, she went upstairs to tell him quietly that she needed to help the police. He was asleep when she opened his bedroom door and she left him a note telling him where she was.

Time dragged at the station. The police went over the same questions time after time. How she wished Paul was with her. He would surely have supported her. It was a pity the police had waited until he'd left before they'd approached her.

'We know all about Rothwell, alias

John Newby. His runners do a good job collecting. But we know he's the big guy, the boss. You must have known his game.' The sergeant was adamant.

'His game? What are you talking about.' She was running out of patience now.

'Credit card fraud. He used one in front of you at *La Rue*. Surely you noticed it wasn't his. We know you were there because we had a report from the restaurant when they discovered a stolen card had been used. You fit the description given to us by the waiter who served you. And now you've confirmed you were there with Newby.'

'Credit card fraud? I doubt it,' she said. 'Simon is a well-to-do business man.'

But then it came back to her. He had been furtive when he'd signed the slip at *La Rue*, but she foolishly thought it was because he didn't want her to see the cost of the meal. She knew it was an expensive restaurant.

Things were starting to add up. The

last time he'd visited her, he'd more or less bragged about having enough money to pay for her.

'That's not the way we see it,' the constable said.

'I know nothing about his criminal activities. Sorry, I can't help you,' she stressed. 'Why would I call you and hand over the credit cards if I was involved?'

'I can see your point, Mrs Henderson. But you were with him at *La Rue*. You must have seen him sign a false name.'

'I'm not in the habit of watching when bills are being paid, credit cards or not. This has nothing whatsoever to do with me. I don't even like the man.'

'That's not the impression we have,' the sergeant sneered. He looked towards the door. 'What is it, constable?'

The constable called him over and whispered. 'It seems your son is here,' the sergeant continued. 'I'm going to release you for now. But stay around.

We'll be back when we've something more concrete to go on. You obviously knew we were on to Newby. You panicked and brought the cards in to save your own neck.'

'What rubbish,' she replied. 'You'll never have anything concrete on me. I'm not involved. Understand?' she said, anger bubbling up inside her as, holding herself erect she walked from the interview room. How dare they?

Josh was there in the waiting room. 'Mum, what's happened?' he asked her, his voice filled with urgency.

'They've got it all wrong, Josh,' she told him. 'Let's get out of here. I'll tell you on the way back.'

Once back at the house Carol started to explain everything to Josh. 'And when they'd finished they had the nerve to suggest I'm in cahoots . . . ' and then she stopped mid-sentence. 'You know it's just occurred to me that I forgot to mention I'd telephoned the real Simon Rothwell at *Fast Gear*. Why would I phone him if I knew the score, if I was involved in this cloning business?'

Without another word she picked up the telephone and dialled the police station, asking to speak with the sergeant.

'It didn't occur to me to mention that I'd rung the company in Nottingham and spoken to the real Simon Rothwell. Ring him and check my story. I'm sure the man was as puzzled as I was when I mentioned the credit cards.'

'Leave it with me, Mrs Henderson. We'll check the story out,' he said. 'You should have mentioned this when you were at the station.'

'Sergeant, I've just told you it slipped my mind,' she replied, unsure as to whether or not she'd convinced the inspector.

But what she couldn't understand was why this John Newby had used Simon Rothwell's name and how he'd managed to obtain full knowledge of the company, *Fast Gear*. He'd certainly convinced her that he was the real Simon Rothwell and that he did run the company *Fast Gear*. And even more convincing was his story about Julie Rothwell as though she really was his wife.

* ★ * ★ * ★ *

Rick Golding explained the wide range of potential to Carol during their meeting, but despite his optimism she was still reluctant to give up her work with Barron and Weeks. The job was her mainstay.

But just a day later she was bombarded with work. Rick came up with a commission for a card company and Guy came back for more pictures.

It was then she decided she must take the gamble and give up her fulltime job completely. She couldn't do everything. And not only was the painting more lucrative, it was more enjoyable too.

She took her coffee into the studio and began to make preparations. 'You're starting early this morning,

165

Mum. Any chance I could have a lift to college. I'm a bit late.'

Carol laughed. 'I don't know, Josh Henderson. You will stay out late,' she said, placing her brushes back on the easel. 'Who is she anyway?'

'How do you mean, Mum?' Josh retorted, his face taking on a rosy hue.

'I suppose you'll tell me when you feel like it,' Carol replied, smiling to herself and thinking how Josh was changing. She'd worried that he lacked confidence, but he'd obviously plucked up the courage to ask a girl out.

After dropping him off, Carol returned to the house and made a fresh cup of coffee before resuming her painting.

But it wasn't long before the door bell rang. She looked out the window. There was a strange car outside and she couldn't see who was standing on the door step. She huffed. Would she ever get started?

Before she had the chance to go downstairs, the door bell rang again.

'I'm coming,' she called out. Someone was impatient. The bell rang again. She opened the door, ready to make a joke of it, but she was glued to the spot. It was Simon.

He pushed past her and slammed the door. 'Thank goodness you're in,' he said. 'The credit cards, the ones I dropped in here, I need them.'

'The police have them,' she replied. 'And I don't know what your game is, but they seem to think I'm involved too.'

He gave a mirthless laugh. 'Miss High and Mighty being involved? That's a joke.' He took hold of her shoulders and pressed her against the wall. 'What else have you told them?'

'You're hurting me, Simon. Stop it.,' she said and tried to shrug herself away. 'What could I tell them? All I know is the pack of lies you gave me. If you hadn't lied to me I'd have been able to return your credit cards to the company.'

'To the company?'

'That was the idea.'

'I see.'

'That was when I thought you had a company. But the police have told me otherwise.'

'Good for them,' he sneered and then he shook her shoulders. 'Any more contact with the police and you'll have me to answer to.'

Suddenly he released her, moved to the door and opened it. 'You do understand, don't you?' He placed his finger on his lips and struck a menacing pose. 'Button it.' He slammed the door behind him and left.

Carol dropped the latch, relief surging through her. Unable to breathe, she struggled for air. How she wished Paul was there to protect her.

Seconds later she heard voices outside and the sound of scuffling on the drive. She daren't open the door. Instead she dashed into the lounge and looked through the window.

The police were there. They'd obviously followed Newby and now they were arresting him.

One of the officers had his hand on Newby's head bundling him into a police car.

There was a knock on the door. It was the sergeant. 'Are you all right? We saw what happened. Did Newby threaten you?'

'Yes. He seems to think I reported the cards maliciously. I tried to explain all I wanted was to return them, but he seemed to think there was more to it than that.'

'You'll be fine now. Don't worry. We have him. But you're not off the hook yet. We'll still need you down at the station once we have the truth out of him.' The sergeant turned as the door opened once more. It was Josh. 'What's going on, Mum. We're not in trouble again I hope.'

'Nothing like that, love. They've caught Simon — John Newby to give him his rightful name.'

'Are you all right, Mum. You don't look it.'

'He gave me a scare. But I'm fine now. The police have taken care of things.

* * *

It was two days before the police sergeant called on Carol again. 'We've had the real Simon Rothwell on the phone. He's confirmed your story, love,' he said, averting his eyes in embarrassment. 'He's been into the station and we've discovered the link. Apparently Newby once worked for his company as a sales rep and thought he could make a bit on the side. Rothwell found out and sacked him. And, according to Rothwell, it's not the first time Newby's used his name. But we have the measure of him now. Sorry you were under suspicion, love, but you must realise we have to explore every avenue.'

'Of course I understand, Sergeant. But surely you can see my side of it too being accused of something I know nothing about.'

'I can. But at least we've cleared things up now. Newby confessed. There'll be no need for you to come down to the station. Newby will be sent down for fifteen years, I can guarantee that. Several of his accomplices were identified too, especially when the story hit the headlines. Retailers were vigilant, reported anyone they suspected of using a magnetic card stripe reader in their stores. We had the major part of the jigsaw. All we needed was the final piece. And that was Newby.'

When Josh came back from college the sergeant was leaving. 'Not again, Mum,' he said, glaring at the sergeant.

'It's not what you think, love. It's the end of John Newby,' she told him. 'He's confessed. I must say he was pretty convincing when he told me about his company. You can't tell the genuine ones any more, either that or I'm becoming more gullible the older I get.'

'Don't say that, Mum. If you're gullible, so am I. I'd never have thought it of him.' Josh sat down opposite

Carol. 'But Paul's genuine. I can vouch for that.'

Carol drifted into a dreamy state again.

'By the way, Mum. Are you listening?'

Carol pulled her thoughts together.

'I've been meaning to ask you. Would you mind if Rachael came back from college with me tomorrow? There's a test we need to prepare for, and we thought we'd sort it out together.'

'You did, did you?' Carol smiled. 'Of course it's all right. I'm looking forward to meeting her.'

'Oh, Mum. Nothing formal, please,' he wailed. 'And none of your jokes and acting the fool.' He put his hands over his face. 'What am I letting myself in for?'

They both started to laugh. 'Don't worry,' Carol replied. 'I won't say anything untoward.'

Josh was about to interject when the phone rang. He stretched out and picked it up. 'It's for you, Mum. I think it's your boyfriend,' he said retaliating.

Carol pulled a face. 'How dare you?' she said, taking the phone from him. It was, of course, Paul. Who else could it be?

'Hi, Paul. Excuse the wisecracks.' She laughed. 'Josh is getting his own back. I've just been teasing him about his new girlfriend. That's his way of embarrassing me calling you my boyfriend.'

'I wish,' came the reply. 'Fancy a meal at Bellini's tomorrow night? Can you make it or, dare I ask, have you made arrangements with your friend from the club?'

'Can I make it? I'm desperate,' she said, ignoring the comment about Newby. 'I've done nothing but work non-stop for the last couple of weeks. I need a break.'

'I'll pick you up at seven, if that's OK.'

'Wonderful, Paul. I can't wait.'

* * *

They sat in Bellini's at a table at the back of the restaurant just as they'd done when they'd first met. They'd finished their meal and were almost ready to leave. Outwardly they might have seemed like any other contented couple enjoying an evening together, maybe celebrating. But there was an underlying tension.

Finally Paul braved the question that had obviously been buzzing around in his mind for some time.

'How are things with Mr BMW from the club? I thought you two were an item. And it's just that maybe the two of us could have had a relationship, but you never claimed that was what you wanted.'

'You never intimated you were interested.'

'But you did nothing to encourage me.'

'You're right,' she said, fighting to keep her voice steady. 'That was because you told me you valued your independence. Don't you think I knew that after you left the class? You were ages before you contacted me.'

'How do you mean? You never gave me a chance. You were too taken up with that fitness fanatic, Simon whatever his name is.'

'You must be joking' she replied, taking a sip of her coffee. 'We went to dinner just the once. I wanted to thank him for rescuing me at the gym. He called at the house once. That was it. I never gave him any encouragement.'

'Don't I know he called at the house,' Paul offered, his voice holding a hint of sarcasm. 'That was the night I came to visit. You were standing in the doorway kissing when I arrived. I didn't stay to witness any more. I didn't want to cramp your style. And that's why I didn't visit again.'

Carol was shocked at what he'd told her.

'Paul, there's something I'd like to say to you.' She paused and took a deep breath before she continued. 'When we met I thought there was some sort of chemistry between us. But then I discovered you enjoyed your independence and I backed off. I left you alone. I didn't want you to think I was desperate.'

She gazed into his eyes. 'And then you saw me with Simon and you drew your own conclusions which were entirely wrong. He forced himself on me. But worse still he's now in prison. He's been convicted of credit card fraud.'

'Oh, no, Carol. I hope he wasn't violent. I couldn't bear it if anyone tried to harm you.'

'It was pretty close, but the police caught him before he could threaten me again,' she told him, 'But I'm sorry it's turned out this way, Paul.'

'What are you saying, Carol? Are you telling me there's never been anything between you and this Simon.'

'Of course not. I passed out in the steam room at the club one day and he rescued me. I felt I owed it to him to accept his invitation to dinner. And that's when the trouble with the credit cards started. But enough of that.'

'But my darling, I got it so wrong.' He looked at her anxiously, taking both her hands and drawing her close. He nuzzled her neck and whispered, 'You're all I've wanted for a long time, but I've been reluctant to tell you because I genuinely thought you and Simon were together.'

'Oh, Paul. I thought I'd never love again after I lost Mike, but we have to move on some time. We have to seek happiness, not just for ourselves, but for our children too.'

Gathering his courage, he took stock of her, leaning back in his chair, his blue eyes now as dark as the midnight sky.

'Do I take it you're saying you like me just a little bit?' His eyes were soft and pleading now and a kind of lethargy seemed to settle over her as she silently read his plea. For what seemed like ages they were caught in the delight of the moment.

'Just a little bit,' she said and she smiled into his eyes.

'Then why are we sitting here arguing, when we could be whispering sweet nothings?' He caught her hand, leant across the table and kissed her, bringing a swift surge of colour to her cheeks.

'What are you saying, Paul? Do I take it you believe me now?'

'Not only that my darling, but there's something I must ask you.'

'And what's that?'

'How do you think Josh would feel having a step-father?'

'It depends who the step-father is.'

'Paul Trent, artist, married to Carol Trent, artist. How would that go down?'

'Like a dream, Paul and with his mate, Tom as his step-brother. Couldn't be better. And by the way, I don't need to ask him. I just know.' A feeling of warmth flooded her body and outwardly she glowed.

'D'you reckon that's settled then,' he

said, lifting himself from his chair and taking her in his arms.

He turned and surveyed the other diners in the restaurant.

'Perhaps we'd better wait until we get out of here,' he whispered. 'Giovanni,' he called. 'The bill please.'

THE END

We do hope that you have enjoyed reading this large print book.

Did you know that all of our titles are available for purchase?

We publish a wide range of high quality large print books including:
Romances, Mysteries, Classics
General Fiction
Non Fiction and Westerns

Special interest titles available in large print are:
The Little Oxford Dictionary
Music Book, Song Book
Hymn Book, Service Book

Also available from us courtesy of Oxford University Press:
Young Readers' Dictionary
(large print edition)
Young Readers' Thesaurus
(large print edition)

For further information or a free brochure, please contact us at:
Ulverscroft Large Print Books Ltd.,
The Green, Bradgate Road, Anstey,
Leicester, LE7 7FU, England.
Tel: (00 44) **0116 236 4325**
Fax: (00 44) **0116 234 0205**

Other titles in the
Linford Romance Library:

TO LOVE AGAIN

Catriona McCuaig

Jenny Doyle had always loved her brother in law, Jake Thomas-Harding, but when he chose to marry her sister instead, she knew it was a love that had no future. Now his wife is dead, and he asks Jenny to live under his roof to look after his little daughter. She wonders what the future holds for them all, especially when ghosts of the past arise to haunt them . . .

FINDING THE SNOWDON LILY

Heather Pardoe

Catrin Owen's father, a guide on Snowdon, shows botanists the sites of rare plants. He wants his daughter to marry Taran Davies. But then the attractive photographer Philip Meredith and his sister arrive, competing to be first to photograph the 'Snowdon Lily' in its secret location. His arrival soon has Catrin embroiled in the race, and she finds her life, as well as her heart, at stake. For the coveted prize generates treachery amongst the rivals — and Taran's jealousy . . .

KEEP SAFE THE PAST

Dorothy Taylor

Their bookshop in the old Edwardian Arcade meant everything to Jenny Wyatt and her father. But were the rumours that the arcade was to be sold to a development company true? Jenny decides to organise a protest group. Then, when darkly attractive Leo Cooper enters her life, his upbeat personality is like a breath of fresh air. But as their relationship develops, Jenny questions her judgement of him. Are her dreams of true love about to be dashed?

LEGACY OF REGRET

Jo James

When Liz Shepherd unexpectedly inherits an elderly man's considerable estate, she is persuaded it is in gratitude for her kindness to him. But doubts set in when Steve Lewis, in the guise of a reporter, challenges her good luck. Was there another reason for her legacy? And why is Steve so interested? She comes to regret her inheritance and all its uncertainties — until Steve helps her find the truth and they discover the secret of their past.

RETURN TO HEATHERCOTE MILL

Jean M. Long

Annis had vowed never to set foot in Heathercote Mill again. It held too many memories of her ex-fiancé, Andrew Freeman, who had died so tragically. But now her friend Sally was in trouble, and desperate for Annis' help with her wedding business. Reluctantly, Annis returned to Heathercote Mill and discovered many changes had occurred during her absence. She found herself confronted with an entirely new set of problems — not the least of them being Andrew's cousin, Ross Hadley . . .

THE COMFORT OF STRANGERS

Roberta Grieve

When Carrie Martin's family falls on hard times, she struggles to support her frail sister and inadequate father. While scavenging along the shoreline of the Thames for firewood, she stumbles over the unconscious body of a young man. As she nurses him back to health she falls in love with the stranger. But there is a mystery surrounding the identity of 'Mr Jones' and, as Carrie tries to find out who he really is, she finds herself in danger.